VIRAGO
MODERN CLASSICS
599

Muriel Spark

Muriel Spark (1918–2006) was born in Edinburgh. She wrote many successful novels, including *The Prime of Miss Jean Brodie*, *Memento Mori*, *Loitering with Intent*, *A Far Cry from Kensington* and *Symposium*, as well as poems, short stories, plays, biographies and children's books. For her long career of literary achievement Muriel Spark won international praise and many awards. She was given an honorary doctorate of Letters from a number of universities, London, Edinburgh and Oxford among these, and was made a Dame of the British Empire in 1993.

Books by Muriel Spark

The Comforters
Robinson
Memento Mori
The Bachelors
The Ballad of Peckham Rye
The Prime of Miss Jean Brodie
The Girls of Slender Means
The Mandelbaum Gate
The Public Image
The Driver's Seat
Not to Disturb
The Hothouse by the East River
The Abbess of Crewe
The Takeover
A Far Cry from Kensington
Territorial Rights
Loitering with Intent
The Only Problem
Symposium
Reality and Dreams
Aiding and Abetting
The Finishing School

TERRITORIAL RIGHTS

Muriel Spark

virago

VIRAGO

This edition published by Virago Press in 2014
First published in Great Britain by Macmillan 1979

A CIP catalogue record for this book
is available from the British Library.

ISBN 978-1-84408-965-9

Typeset in Goudy by M Rules
Printed and bound in Great Britain by
Clays Ltd, St Ives plc

Papers used by Virago are from well-managed forests
and other responsible sources.

MIX
Paper from
responsible sources
FSC
www.fsc.org   FSC® C104740

Virago Press
An imprint of
Little, Brown Book Group
100 Victoria Embankment
London EC4Y 0DY

An Hachette UK Company
www.hachette.co.uk

www.virago.co.uk

I

The bureau clerk was telephoning to the Pensione Sofia while Robert Leaver watched the water-traffic at the ferry and the off-season visitors arriving in Venice. It was a sunny day in October. The clerk, having spoken to the Sofia, told him there was a room vacant there. Robert nodded. 'On vacation?' said the bureau man. 'Research. Art History,' said Robert, lifting his briefcase and his suitcase.

He was taken to the Pensione Sofia through the sunny waters of palaces, domes and ferries. It was his first visit to Venice and he was young; but he had only half a mind to feel enchanted, the other half being still occupied with a personal anxiety in Paris from where he had just come. So that, while he was subject to the imperative claims of Venice the beautiful on first sight, he heard still in his ears the impatient voice of the older man: Goodbye, goodbye, goodbye, good-*bye*. Robert had been floundering about his own goodbyes, had made them apologetically, had said too many goodbyes. His suitcase in his hand, Robert had turned on the doorstep. 'I'll get in touch ... goodbye again ... goodbye for now ... well, good—'

'Goodbye, goodbye, goodbye, good*bye*.'

It was as if the older man had said, 'You bore me. You can't even leave in good style. You haven't any slightest savvy about partings. You've always bored me. *Goodbye very much. Goodbye.*'

With this angry memory not far behind, Robert let himself take in Venice, noting everything he passed on the way to the Pensione with a merely photographic attention.

The bright-eyed, plump young porter was waiting for him at the gate ready to take his bags. Robert let go of his suitcase but clung nervously to his briefcase. The porter showed no involvement one way or the other, but proceeded up the short flagged path of the street-entrance to its high glass doorway. The outside walls of the Pensione were flaky but obviously it had been a handsome villa. He followed the porter into a long reception hall. The villa had been converted into a little private hotel. A few people were sitting about, ready to go out, waiting for their friends to come down. There was a large dark television set at the far end of the room with a group of chairs round it emptily waiting for the evening to fall. Behind the television was a wide french window, its curtains open; beyond that a long garden receding from the back of the house.

Two middle-aged women simultaneously detached themselves from the armchairs. One had been knitting, the other reading a magazine. They might have been guests, but they approached the reception desk together, smiling, obliging, and in charge. Their heads, as they bent over the big book to check his room, were alike, yellow-grey, neatly and newly done by the hairdresser. The forefinger of one of the women moved down the page to find his place, the forefinger of the other found it.

One of the good ladies behind the desk was asking, in adequate hotel English, how long he wanted to stay.

He opened his mouth and paused before replying in a French-inclined Italian, 'Two or three weeks. Maybe a month'; and he seemed to have made this decision on the spot; almost, he could have said 'Two or three days. Maybe a week.'

Her fingers moved around in the big book. 'There's a large room with two windows and separate shower, or another room, smaller with full bath.'

'Two windows?' the young man said. 'The room with the bath, has it two windows?'

'No, only one,' Eufemia said. 'I'll show you both rooms.' She reached for the keys.

He followed, inordinately fussed about the choice between the two assets. A room with two windows, and only with shower. A room with one window but a full bath. Goodbye, goodbye. He took the large room with two windows and shower.

'Thank you, signora,' he said, whereupon she invited him to call her Eufemia, adding that her sister was Katerina. And even this made Robert anxious, lest he should have got himself into an over-intimate guest-house, which might threaten his privacy.

'You're lucky to find this room,' Eufemia said as she checked the soap and the towels, and opened the cupboards and drawers to see that all was well for the new visitor. The room was large and randomly furnished with slightly shaky, though shiny, furniture. He noticed a telephone by the bed, and a desk, which for some reason reassured him about his personal independence in the place. 'Even out of season,' Eufemia was saying, 'you'd be surprised how many tourists arrive every day in Venice. Are you on holiday?'

'Research,' he said. 'Art History.'

One of the windows looked out on a garden with the canal beyond, the other had a view of a large square with a bulbous church at the end of it.

'Art history? Good, good!' said Eufemia, as if unique wonders would never cease. 'Well, sir, can I have your passport for the register?'

From the outside, Santa Maria Formosa is a bulbous and comely church. Behind it laps one of the narrow lanes of Venetian water which link streets to churches, squares to alleys. The church is wide and peaceful in its volume as if the front doors opened to show off the square before it, the square and all that stands around, the pharmacy, the funeral shop with its shiny coffins stacked one on top of another and carved with enthusiasm, the uneven roof-line, the Bar Dell'Orologio wherein youth and age stand eyeing each other, and, on the far left, the Communist Party's ornate and ancient headquarters with its painted façade. Standing within the church doors you could, of course, see a short way down the side-path leading from the far end of the square to the street-gate and old-fashioned front garden of the Pensione Sofia.

Robert had come here as soon as he had unpacked, crossing the little bridge of the side-canal to the path that led into the expansive square. It was the afternoon hour when the shops were opening after lunch. Robert had walked around to see what sights there were to save up for later visits, and now was in the bar having coffee and a bun. He was wearing blue jeans and a thick sweater. He was twenty-four, thin, tallish and had a good head of light brown curly hair and a droopy brown moustache. Some other students of both sexes stood in the bar, came and went. Robert showed a piece of paper to the barman. It had an address on it, but the barman, having puzzled over it, said he had never heard of it. He then asked where this address was, which question was not really stupid; the other Venetians who now joined in with Robert's problem made it clear that they knew where every place in their city was, but they didn't know the streets by names. Where was this address near to, what monument, what bridge, what shop, what church? Was it up or down the Grand Canal from the Rialto Bridge? Another student, a Canadian, presently recognized the name of the street; this led to further discussion and finally it was marked on Robert's map; not really very far away from where he was.

It was the moment that he came out of the bar that Robert caught a glimpse away in the distance of Lina Pancev, the girl whose address he was looking for. It was by her outline that he recognized her unmistakably, for she dressed in a gypsy style, bulky with full gathered skirts and shawls, more common among the young of Paris than of Venice. With this, she walked with a certain sway, more proud than really sexy. Her small head, with black bobbed hair, was set to look straight ahead with a touch of rigidity, as usual. She was crossing the far end of a narrow street leading off the Campo di Santa Maria Formosa. Her head and her outline passed and were lost.

Robert hurried to catch up with her, negotiating the mothers, prams, children on wild skateboards, students, old men and tourists who were filling the square in the last hours of sunlight. She had gone from sight when he reached the end of the narrow street, but he took the route towards her address and eventually, by the side of the bridge, in a narrow aperture between two high palaces, he saw her again standing there. She looked around her briefly, but only in her immediate vicinity, as if to assure herself that no one could physically stop her from some projected action, rather like a market-thief about to steal a bunch of grapes. Then she bent to lift her voluminous skirt to the knees, and shook out from under it an empty mackerel-tin, a milk-carton, bits of egg-shell and some pieces of old lettuce. She kicked aside this garbage, then walked on to her destination. It was exactly what she had done the day Robert had first seen her in a mean little side-street in Paris. That first time she had looked up and seen the young man watching her, and laughed, although she was embarrassed too. Robert had said, in an easy young way, 'What are you doing?'

She had said she was getting rid of her garbage. Apparently, she lodged in a cheap room where she wasn't allowed to cook. Well, she couldn't afford to eat out, so she cooked all the same on a spirit-stove that she carried about with her from place to place. She managed quite well, she explained, the only problem being how to get rid of the rubbish; and she solved the problem by stuffing it up her clothes and shedding it in a back-street. She said, 'I have to wear the big old women's pants that come to the knees.' She spoke first in French, and then changed to English because, as she explained to Robert later, he was laughing in English.

This time Robert didn't laugh. He stood where he was, staring at the mystery of this exact repetition of events in another city; it was a near-hallucination, and, after all, it was no mystery, for Lina obviously had taken the same sort of poor lodgings and settled in with her forbidden spirit-stove. He had known Lina now for six weeks. First Paris and now Venice; goodbye, good*bye*. Lina was now out of sight, but he walked on after her to her new address.

It seemed that the trouble between the two was about the autumn leaves.

Robert, watching at the garden window of his room, looked down on the neat heads of the two women.

The garden, dotted with rose-beds and other bright flowers, was divided by a gravel pathway about three feet wide. All down the exact middle of this path was set a row of whitewashed stones; they looked like those put on mountain roads to warn of a deep cliff-edge. Now the two women stood one on each side of the dividing line, stoutly, with one toe apiece precisely touching the verge. By the side of one of the women lay a mound of bright leaves; it was a huge mound, turning damp at the base, evidently intended for compost. It could have looked glorious to Robert in the faint misty light of that afternoon had his mind been more his own.

The two proprietors of the establishment shrieked on, not in the Italian they used when speaking to clients, but in a Venetian dialect of which the witness at the window could have perceived here and there only a few familiar landmarks of rational discourse. The argument turned on the actual place where the fallen leaves had been piled up. The leaves themselves seemed to be the responsibility of the one called Katerina. A few of them had accidentally spilled over the white line into that part of the garden where Eufemia, the other, was standing. Presently the violence and tone of the flare-up in the garden subsided into low grumbles, and then into nothing.

This was two days after Robert's arrival. The afternoon sky had turned grey. He heard the water-traffic of Venice behind the shrubbery, at the far end of the garden path. There was movement, too, on the side-canal and on the little bridge which led to the footpath and to the river-gate of the Pensione Sofia. After the women's voices had dissolved, Robert, still watching at the window, saw only the one called Eufemia standing her ground, in silence. She wore a sensible skirt and one of her stockings was slightly askew. On the other side of the white boundary, the other, Katerina, having reluctantly conceded the battle, bent to pick up in little handfuls the stray leaves; she threw them on to the vivid pile on the side where she stood and achieved this without placing her foot over the boundary. At one point, when three spreadeagled sprays of foliage seemed too far away for Katerina to reach, Eufemia pushed them nearer to hand with her shoe.

They went into the house then, the joint proprietors, who apparently spent most of the time in harmony downstairs in the large hall at the entrance, watching the television, gossiping with the guests, or hastening to the reception desk to check in a new arrival and show them their rooms. Sometimes as Robert passed in and out Eufemia was alone behind the desk, totting up accounts or answering the telephone; at other times both of them were busy there together, one putting straight the picture postcards on their racks and the other supplying a guest as it might be with a postage stamp or a travel pamphlet. On these occasions they were so equally amiable to all and to each other as to be almost interchangeable.

After the women had gone indoors Robert continued to contemplate the empty garden for a little space, then shook himself out of his idleness and turned back to his room.

On the last lap of his journey from Paris, Mark Curran drove across the causeway on the approach to Venice, the water-flats of the lagoon spreading on either side in a fading light. Mark Curran had come to settle things with Robert; he was rich in substance and experience, a man of sixty-two, with settled, sophisticated tastes and few doubts.

He preferred to be called 'Curran' rather than by his Christian name, for reasons which, when he gave them, were difficult to puzzle out – as, for instance, that he hated anyone to pity him or feel that he ever needed pity. From this it was presumably to be supposed that to call him 'Mark' might conceivably lay him open, at some given time, to be offered sympathy.

His being known as 'Curran' to his friends and 'Mr Curran' to passing acquaintances had a curious effect on his relationships with women. For, unless the women were very young and free, or else tough like those older ones who rang him up and said, 'Oh, is that you, Curran?' (as if he were the butler), most women stuck to 'Mr Curran', and this kept them rather far away. In fact, Curran's simple phrase, cast off in earnest jollity, 'I prefer my friends just to call me Curran,' had many strange effects on his life. It forced the men he met socially to always treat him in a man-to-man style: 'My dear Curran, I'm passing thro' Paris ...' And 'Yours, Curran,' he would sign his letters, no matter how much he wrote to Dear James, Dear Arthur or Dear Robert.

He drove into Venice very much aware of being Curran. He knew Venice well; it had been his territory for the best part of his life, in the late thirties and after the war onwards, when he had become a settled expatriate. He returned once a year to the United States to see a few ageing members of his family and attend to those things that had to be attended to. Paris was his headquarters from where he drove around when a change was called for. He was often in London, often in the South of France, often in Capri, sometimes Florence and less frequently nowadays, in Rome. He hardly ever went to Germany unless to buy a picture and he left Switzerland alone. Venice was very much his territory; it changed less than other places with the passing of time.

With time and its passing much on his mind, and, as always, full of the Curran idea, he left his car at the terminus and took a water-taxi to the Hotel Lord Byron.

At the back of the Campo di Santa Maria Formosa was a network of streets and narrow gutter-canals, at high tide smelling like dead fish and at low tide even worse. The befouled water lapped at the lower doors of the tall buildings on either side; but these doors had been closed for ever. The entrances to the buildings were round the other side, in some narrow alley between the waterways.

Lina Pancev lived in a room perched at the top of one of these narrow houses. From the street, this room projected like a large bird, a dangerous-looking piece of masonry, yet not dangerous presuming the bird could fly. The beak protruding from its small window was at this moment devoid of its washing, and the small black mouth was shut, unlike the windows underneath it, set further back into the building. To reach the hovering attic it was necessary to climb, in the first place, five twisting flights of stairs, each step of which was worn to a thin curve in the centre. The iron banister, wrought in curly patterns on the lower floors, soon became a rusty twisting strip, too shaky and broken to depend upon. The sight and smell of rats, cats and garbage at the entrance changed, as the climber proceeded, to the smell of something or other more frightful. Then, with the staircase left behind, came the testing part, the challenge: a pair of builders' planks about three feet in length led from the landing, itself slanting by quite a few degrees, across to the threshold of Lina Pancev's eyrie. What had been there before the planks were laid would have puzzled any architect; the building was at least three centuries old, and the planks themselves looked as if they had been there for at least ten years; and how the jutting room where Lina lived defeated the law of gravity to the functional extent it did, perhaps not even the original constructors had known. The building had been many years condemned by the authorities, but was fully inhabited; its dim and puddly privies on every landing were vital evidence of the tenants' presence.

Robert Leaver, crossing the planks to Lina's door, could not resist looking down through the slit between them, as he had done on his first visit. The planks were springy; a sheer long drop to the narrow street below. He rang the bell which always astonishingly not only worked, but did so by electricity. 'Who is it?' called Lina in Italian. 'It's me,' said Robert in English. She opened the door and let him into her lamplit room.

'Did you bring your torch?' she said.

'Oh, I forgot it again!'

'I'll have to take you down with mine when you go.' Dusk was falling and there was nothing to light the uncharitable staircase but an occasional slit-window on a landing. 'I'll have to go down with you and then climb all the way back. The batteries are expensive.'

But she didn't seem to notice that her greeting to Robert was no sort of greeting at all. He accepted it in a casual dazed way, plainly thinking of something far more pressing. Inside the room he had to walk downhill to a heavy armchair, with many cotton cushions and broken springs, more or less tethered to the slope. Robert sat lop-sided like a paralytic and told Lina that Curran had arrived in Venice. 'He phoned me up out of the blue,' Robert said.

'Blue?' she said. She looked at her plain wood worktable: a folded painting-book; paint-brushes soaking in a jam-jar half-full of grey water.

'Unexpectedly,' he said sulkily.

'Oh, you must have given him your number,' Lina said, 'or else how could he find you?'

'Curran wouldn't find that difficult; and in this case all he had to do was to get the hall porter at his hotel to ring up the obvious places. In any case Curran's used to finding people.'

'Then in that case, maybe he can find my dead father.'

'He might do that,' said Robert.

'Good,' she said, really taking him up on it.

'You seem very delighted,' he said, 'to know that Curran's here.'

'Well,' she said, 'I'm not in rivalry never with no one. I told you that.'

'You'd like to use Curran,' he said.

'Why not, if he could be useful?'

'Curran paints too, you know,' Robert said. 'I'm no judge,

but he sells his paintings. They're abstract in oils. He gets a lot of money for them.'

'Who from? His fancy friends?'

'Exclusively, his friends. Nobody else goes to his shows.'

'It happened also in Bulgaria like that,' she said. 'But there I had a lot of friends, myself.' She was very placid, not in the least resentful of Curran, as were two other professional artists whom Robert knew in Paris. She was clearing part of the table. 'My friends were poor but Curran's are rich.' It was like a piece from a nursery-rhyme.

She was arranging her spirit-stove on top of a wooden fruit-crate. She filled a cooking-pot with water from a big old-fashioned jug, and put it on the stove to heat.

'Tell me the whole story,' she said, with warm comfort in her voice.

'Not at all,' he said. 'Don't be so ambitious.'

'I don't pay rent any more,' she told him, following some sequence of her own thoughts. 'Friday was my rent day, but I've stopped paying because my neighbours have asked me to join them in a strike. We live in a condemned building, so he has no right to rent the rooms. He's angry. It was so little rent, but I am showing solidarity.' She adjusted the flame. ' . . . with my neighbours,' she said, poising the dry spaghetti above the pot, ready to send it in as soon as the water came to the boil. 'And I can do my cooking if I want to because everyone else does. From today I don't smuggle out the rubbish. I put it in the canal like the other people, when there's no police boat coming up.'

Robert watched her while she cooked; a smaller pot, onions, peeled tomatoes from a tin, a drop of oil, another drop. Her black hair had a high shine, with its short bob and fringe; it was the sort of hair that hairdressers loved to handle, and looked expensively cut, although this was unlikely. She had apple-red cheeks and white teeth, looking very Balkan, like one of the tourist-shops' Dolls of All Nations. He liked her unscrupulous story about the rent; in fact, he agreed with her about the rent in one sense as much as he disagreed in another. At his universities he had known girls without materialistic scruples, as they put it. His mother had strict scruples; what's mine is mine and what's yours is yours.

Lina's voice chattered on. Eventually he said, 'What was that you said, Lina?'

'You haven't been listening.'

'Yes, I have. I just didn't catch—'

'What was I talking about?'

'You said "eggs". – What about the eggs?'

She attended to her paraffin-stove, moving her two pots, the big and the small, alternately over the flame. She said, 'I said that this is all I've got to offer you. Tomorrow I'll go out and get some *eggs*.'

'It's very good of you,' he said. 'You're a lovely woman, too.'

'I'm tired,' she said. 'When are you seeing Curran?'

'Tomorrow, in the evening.'

Tomorrow, in the evening, Robert walked through the lanes and across the bridges, under the clear stars and over their reflection in the waters, to Harry's Bar, took a place downstairs and waited. The older man, when he arrived, looked more opulent than usual, appearing very much like a rich elder friend of a nice good-looking, lean young student.

'Well, Robert,' said Curran, 'nice to see you again. A bit of luck I found you in Venice.'

'It was a bit of luck,' said the young man blithely.

'Ever eaten here before?' Curran said, even though he knew Harry's Bar was beyond Robert's pocket, and that this was the young man's first visit to Venice.

'I've found a moderate restaurant,' Robert said firmly. 'And there are snack bars.'

'Oh yes, of course. Well, we can make a more spectacular meal tonight if you feel it would be a change. I've booked a table upstairs. First of all, what will you drink?' They sat at a table near the bar.

Around them was the buzz and small-clatter of multifarious activities, such as the shuffling of chairs and feet, the conversations at the bar and at the other tables, the sound of the door swinging open with the entrance of new arrivals and the constant clink of bottles and glasses at the bar. It made a good environment for their meeting. Robert was relieved that Curran had not asked him to come somewhere quiet, and it did not occur to him now, as they waited for their whiskies, that in fact he need not have come at all.

'What brings you to Venice?' he said, invitingly, to Curran.

'Force of will,' Curran said, as if there had been no 'Goodbye, goodbye, good*bye*' and no shouting recriminations leading up to it.

Curran said, 'What about your studies?'

'I can do history of art here as well as I can in Paris. Perhaps better. Venetian architecture and art. I can switch.'

'How?'

'You can arrange it for me,' Robert said. 'I can switch my grant and do a term paper in Venice.'

Curran laughed, and said, 'Were you counting on me to come and arrange things for you?'

'I suppose, maybe, I was.'

'Exactly what aspect of Venice would you undertake? I'm sure I wouldn't be able to decide if I were in your place. And you'd be surprised how much I know Venice. I was here as a young man. I was here at the end of the war. I couldn't tell you the number of times, off and on ... and yet, where would one begin?'

'If you had to begin, you'd begin.'

'I dare say. Sheer force of will would do it. I've done some of my best paintings in Venice, but of course that's rather a different thing.'

'Well,' said Robert, 'when you begin to deal with a subject, you gather as many details as possible, then you find the features general to all of them, and you develop the generalities.'

'Very enlightening,' said Curran, 'so far as it goes. But you've described a lifetime's occupation if you're going to do it thoroughly, and you haven't been here a week. Will you have another drink or shall we go upstairs?'

They went up to dinner. Robert said, 'I'm starting off with Santa Maria Formosa. It's a curvaceous building, most unusual.'

'Oh, yes, I know it. What made you pick on that?'

'It's the first thing I saw when I walked out of the Pensione. I might as well begin there. I've looked it up in the library.

There are some vague legends about the name, but my thesis is that the name of Santa Maria Formosa originally came from the "formosa" of the Song of Solomon in the Bible. Original Latin: *Nigra sum sed formosa* – "I am black but comely." It was a prefiguration of the Madonna according to the early theologians. Now as it happens I have discovered that the ancient Hebrew could mean "black but comely" or "beautiful" or "shapely" and it could also mean "black *and* comely", or again it could mean "black, *therefore* comely". So I intend to write a thesis ... '

Curran held up his hand to indicate the waiter standing by the table. 'We'd better order,' Curran said.

And when they had ordered he said, 'Go on.'

'Are you bored?' Robert said.

'Your thesis should be popular,' said Curran.

'That's what it seemed to me.'

'I should say you've done a lot of thinking in quite a short time.'

'Oh, yes,' Robert said, 'I've done that.'

'I should say the church might well be named merely after its own shape. Quite simply that,' said Curran. 'Talking about shape, you haven't told me about the girl.'

'Which girl?'

'How many are there?'

'Only one that matters.'

'She's dangerous. Keep away from her.'

'Is that what you've come to tell me?'

'Yes. Lina Pancev, daughter of Victor Pancev whom I knew before the war, a Bulgarian. He was suspected of being part of a plot to poison King Boris, who in fact died of poisoning. Pancev got away, but the Bulgarian royalists caught up with him and killed him in 1945. That was your woman-friend's father.'

'Well, it was a long time ago. I wasn't born.'

'But the daughter was. She's no youngster compared to you.'

'Nor are you, compared to her.'

'I don't enter into it. I've only come to tell you that this woman's dangerous. She's a defector from Bulgaria and it seems to me she's being followed. How is your steak?'

'What?'

'What you're eating. Is it done all right?'

'Yes, it's all right. I don't notice what I'm eating.'

'You young people don't. Well, she's being followed by agents of some sort, probably Balkan. They don't like people slipping away.'

'Look, she's only a little nobody to them—'

Curran said, 'She was on a group visit with some Bulgarian art teachers in Paris last year, and she left the group. They're after her.'

'The Paris police know all about her. She's got asylum,' Robert said. 'All in order.'

'How do you know?'

'Well, what's it got to do with me? She's looking for her father's grave here in Venice, and I'm helping her.'

'We're talking in circles. You're in danger if you're seen with her.'

'You mean,' said Robert, 'I'm in danger of losing your

friendship if I'm seen with her. Do you think I'm afraid? I've got a right to have a girl. You think I'm effeminate?'

'Don't raise your voice like that. We're probably being overheard, anyway.'

'You think me effeminate. I've told you I refuse to be labelled,' Robert said.

'I think you masculine to a fault,' said Curran.

Robert looked round the room. The other diners were all of them in parties, intent on their talking and eating, their ordering and their drinking, laughing, smiling. They looked as if they had nothing else but their own lives on their minds, and on their well-dressed bodies, no virtue so penetrating even as an eavesdropping device. On the other hand, look again: maybe everybody, every single diner, could be capable of extending his range. The place could be filled with spies, how could one tell?

'You know,' said Robert, 'I don't believe what you're saying. I don't believe she's being followed. I think it's a cheap trick you've thought up.'

'What for?' said Curran. 'Why? Why should I take trouble for you?' He looked round the room. 'As it happens,' he said, 'those people who keep following you and Lina Pancev are not here tonight. I hardly thought they would be.'

'It gets me down,' said Robert, 'the way you look around as if you owned the place.'

'How you nag!' said Curran. 'Just like a middle-class wife.'

'What's wrong with the middle class,' Robert said, 'apart from people like you?'

'Men like you,' said Curran, 'is what's wrong with the

middle class. The English public schools used to make heroes; nowadays they turn out Hamlets.'

'If you don't like men like me,' Robert sniped, 'then what are you doing in Venice?'

After dinner they walked briskly through the chilly lanes and squares, where the side-canals were ill-lit and the future beyond every few steps was murky. 'Easy . . .' said Curran, as practically every visitor to Venice says, sooner or later, 'very easy – wouldn't it be? – to slither a knife into someone, push him into the canal and just walk on.' At which Robert looked at Curran in a startled way, so that Curran laughed.

A motor-barge could be heard approaching from a side-canal ahead of them. 'That's the port authority,' Curran said. A smooth-sounding motor followed it. 'That's the water police,' said Curran.

'You look good,' said Curran.

'Go to hell.'

Robert had found Curran in the front hall of the Pensione Sofia, seated at a table with Katerina and Eufemia. It was mid-morning. Robert had come in the front door with the English newspaper in his hand, and there was Curran chatting away as if he had known the women all his life.

The women dispersed discreetly as Curran got up to greet Robert. And 'Go to hell,' Robert said when Curran came out with, 'You look good.'

'But you looked bad yesterday,' Curran said. 'Something on your mind, no doubt.' Equable, gradual, encompassing, Curran looked around him, owning the place with his manner. 'In daylight,' he said, 'the interior of this house has always been enchanting. That staircase ...' He let his eyes muse on the staircase.

'You know the house, then,' Robert stated. It was inevitable that Curran should know the house. And in fact Curran then said, 'If one has knocked about Europe as long as I have, one does tend to know places.'

'I've got an appointment,' Robert said, looking at his watch.

Regardless, Curran said, 'It was owned by a Bulgarian count up to the beginning of the war. In those days it was the Villa Sofia.' He still looked up the staircase; it was wide with well-worn shabby carpets, and Curran gazed as if to say, 'I remember when it was a private villa and I was a young man coming down, going up, those stairs.' Above the staircase was an old, well-preserved chandelier; it was three-tiered, made of white Dresden china, the top tier portraying pineapples and shepherdesses, and the other two tiers being fully occupied by electric-bulbed candelabras, elaborately ivied. 'That was here in those days,' Curran said. 'It was imported to replace a Venetian glass chandelier. We found it rather comical, among ourselves.' And, as usual, Curran didn't say who were 'we' and 'ourselves', thus leaving Robert far away beyond the scope of one of the many worlds that Curran pervaded and seemed to own.

And indeed, like a proprietor, Curran said, 'Let's go out through the garden and round to the landing-stage. When will you be free? Can we lunch?'

'Are you sure visitors are allowed in the garden?' Robert said. 'It looks like their private garden.'

Curran said, 'I know them well. Katerina and Eufemia are old friends.' He was already at the french windows, followed by Robert. 'And lunch?' Curran said.

'I've promised to take Lina to the island of San Michele today. San Michele is the cemetery island. She's looking for the place where her father's buried.'

'You won't find him there,' Curran said, stepping into the winter sunlight. Robert followed him.

'Have you any idea where he's buried?' Robert said.

Curran said, 'He's buried in his friends' memory. Isn't that enough?'

The compost of dying leaves had gone from the place where the women had stood quarrelling in a high-pitched battle over the heap. Probably the leaves had been carted to the end of the garden earlier that morning, and burned; certainly, the smoky smell of autumn fires, from one garden or another, hung about the air they breathed.

They walked down the gravel path which divided the pretty garden. Robert told how he had seen and heard the two good ladies quarrelling, each on her own side of the garden. Curran seemed interested in this, and sadly amused. 'I believe they've shared everything equally all their lives,' he said.

Robert said, 'You know a lot; too much. I don't trust this place.'

'It's a perfectly good place. The best value in Venice.'

Robert said, 'Out here one would hardly know one was in Venice.' But he looked beyond the railings and the trees, where Venice could be seen, sure enough. Tips of houses, bell-towers and a strange chimney-pot rose on the skyline at the end of the garden, beyond the side-canal, beyond the tops of buildings; they rose in sunlight from the noisy cold canals. To the people walking about, across the bridges, down the narrow streets and across the squares it was everyday life, devoid of tourists, capricious as the sun; to the people going to work it was a day of dull routine and bright weather, boring, cold and quite normally inconvenient.

A water-taxi was approaching up the side-canal; its engine changed rhythm as it chugged into the side, to slow up at the landing-stage of the house. It held two passengers, a man and a woman, both standing, now, getting ready to disembark. Robert gave a shiver some seconds before he really saw these people, probably because he had not slept well and so was specially intuitive. He took Curran's arm and held it tight, so that Curran started with alarm, as if afraid of some violent attack from Robert.

By now the man was standing up and stepping ashore. He was a good five feet away. An elderly man, tall, exceedingly neat, slightly bent at the shoulders, with spectacles and a white-yellow moustache which was small and well cut. He in turn had recognized Robert. His companion, a woman of middle-age wearing a golden-brown fur-coat and tight boots, and, like the man, very neat about the head, said clearly enough to be heard by Robert and Curran, 'What's the matter?'

The man did not reply. He stared, with his lips forming a gasp, very much resembling Robert in his aghast expression.

'Almighty God!' Robert said in a low voice. 'That's my father.'

'What's he doing here?' said Curran.

'I haven't the faintest idea.'

'And is that his friend?'

'I have only the faintest idea who she might be.'

'Evidently he has a lady-friend,' Curran said. 'No harm in that.'

The elderly man stepped ashore leaving his companion to be helped by the taxi-man. The motor-boat swayed as their luggage was unloaded.

In some embarrassment the father said, over the hedge which separated them, 'Robert! what are you doing here? I thought you were in Paris.'

The woman looked at Robert with a social smile which seemed out of place in the open air, but somehow showed willing. But Robert's father was agitated. 'What are *you* doing here?' Robert said.

Meanwhile, the porter had arrived to pick up their luggage and carry it into the house. Robert said, 'We'd better go back indoors. It's the only way.'

'Try to be friendly to them,' Curran said. 'What have you got to worry about?'

They went back through the garden door, emerging in the hall just as the couple were being escorted to the front desk. 'Well, Dad,' said Robert, 'this is a surprise.'

The father gave a childish sort of laugh and looked round the room as if wanting to say he had not come ashore from the water-taxi; he had not arrived in Venice; it was all a mistake. But his woman-friend stood there by his side, solid and indissoluble. 'A little holiday,' he said. 'My former colleague and I are having a little holiday. Here in Venice.'

'Oh, your colleague . . . ' said Robert, with the cruellest of courtesy. The elderly man suddenly gave his son a look of disgust.

Robert introduced his companion in a vague sort of way which obliged Curran to pronounce his own name as he shook hands with Robert's father and his woman companion. 'This is my friend . . . ' Robert had said. His father, Arnold Leaver, was more explicit in return. 'Arnold Leaver,' he said, 'and my colleague Mary Tiller – my son Robert, he was at Ambrose before, your day, Mary, and Mr . . .?'

'Curran,' Curran repeated, with pronounced breath-with-holding, restraint in his voice. 'D'y'-do,' he murmured, his eyes half-closed in keeping with his half-closed voice.

'Well, Robert,' said his father, 'I thought you were in Paris. What brings you here?'

'Research,' said Robert.

He looked hard at his father, in an effort not to look hard at the woman. He had been told his father had this rich mistress but he had never seen her. She said, 'What a coincidence! We must meet later. Let's get this desk business over and unpack our things.'

'Two singles,' Robert's father was demanding at the desk as if it was a railway station.

'Leaver? – We have a booking for a double room. There is the grand bridal suite: bedroom, dressing-room and bathroom.'

Curran withdrew discreetly, but Robert did not.

'There must have been a mistake,' said Arnold Leaver. 'I reserved single rooms, for Mrs Tiller and for myself.'

'There is one single room for Leaver, already taken,' said the perplexed lady at the desk, who happened to be Eufemia. She was joined, then, by Katerina, who bent her head likewise over the ledger. 'Leaver,' said Katerina, pointing a finger to the place; both she and Eufemia pronounced the name 'Leàver'.

Robert, who was close beside his father and companion at the other side of the desk, put in, 'I'm the Leaver in that room. This is my father Mr Arnold Leàver and Mrs Tiller who both want single rooms.'

'We have single rooms on different floors, will that do?' Katerina said. She looked suspicious but tolerant. She said, 'We have a double room booked for a Mr and Mrs Leàver.'

'Those single rooms will do,' said Robert's father. He pulled out his passport and Mary Tiller coolly revealed that her passport was packed away in her luggage. There and then she opened one of her pieces of matched luggage to produce it, in spite of the two proprietors' protests that she could bring it down later, at her convenience. Meantime, Robert noticed that his father's well-worn passport was a double one, made out in the names of Arnold Leaver, colour of eyes grey, colour of hair grey, and his wife Anthea, colour of eyes blue, colour of hair fair. He couldn't see the photographs on the passport from where he stood, but Mrs Tiller's eyes and hair corresponded well enough with those attributed to the absent Anthea. She was not unlike Anthea, a younger Anthea and more flamboyant. That's typical, Robert thought. He leaves one woman for another practically the same.

'Here you are!' Mary Tiller said with a perceptible look of triumph towards Robert, defying his thought with her common cheeriness, so unlike his mother's. She held out the passport, open on the name-and-address page, while handing it over the counter, so that Robert, if he wanted, could clearly see that she had her own. Robert looked away at something vaguely else, then turned his head towards his father. 'Anyone would think,' he said with nasty geniality, 'that you were travelling as man and wife. Double passport – double room booked . . .'

'How could you say such a thing?' said the father in a hushed and beautiful tone, as if Robert had committed something reproachable in church. 'It's not funny,' he said. 'It could be embarrassing, their inefficiency, if there was anything to be embarrassed about, which of course there isn't.'

'How could you have done such a thing?' Curran said. He was standing with Robert in a bar near the Rialto Bridge, taking a coffee. Curran said, 'It was a horrible sight – the way you embarrassed your father. It was also very indiscreet, very uncivilized and, in the civilized sense, unnatural.'

'I meant it,' Robert said.

'That's my point,' Curran said. 'Positively destructive. We have enough difficulties without creating unnecessary antagonism.'

'Speak for yourself.'

'Why?' said Curran. 'Why should I? If I choose to speak for

us both, after all this time, I'll do it. Your father turns up with his colleague—'

'Colleague!' said Robert. 'She used to be a cook.'

'As a matter of fact she was a colleague. As a matter of fact,' Curran said, 'I know something about your father's career at Ambrose College. Mrs Tiller is your father's mistress, naturally, but she was also his colleague, which is to say in a courteous way he preferred to style her a colleague rather than a subordinate, since she was on the staff at Ambrose. She taught cooking, an unusual experiment for a boys' school, but successful. At first she visited three evenings a week to give lessons in cooking to five boys; and very soon her class increased to twenty-odd. When your father retired last year she gave three months' notice and left the school within two. A woman of fairly independent means. An excellent cook. The school will have difficulty replacing her I should think.'

'You seem to know a lot. You know too much. How can you know all this about my father?'

'Money,' said Curran. 'Just money. Like buying a tie, or a plane ticket to Hong Kong, one can buy information about people's fathers.'

He picked up his bill from the counter. 'And so on,' he said.

They left the café and stood at the landing-stage waiting for a water-bus.

'To my mind,' nagged Curran, 'it was infantile, the way you hung around that reception desk, making so much embarrassment for the couple. You dislike your father – all right—'

'I don't dislike him,' Robert said. 'Only I was upset by seeing him here in Venice at this moment of my life, naturally. And I don't approve of his travelling around with his so-called colleague, using my mother's share of the passport.'

'Your mother should have had a separate passport. It's the best, the most sensible way, these days.'

'Oh well, my mother isn't like that. She never travels abroad alone.'

A water-bus arrived. They watched, with automatic blank-faced attentiveness, the faces of the people who were getting off at this stop. Robert embarked with the waiting crowd. Curran walked away.

2

The luxury-class Hotel Lord Byron, which never closed out of season, on the water-front of the Grand Canal, was a Renaissance ducal palace. The interior had been converted at the end of the nineteenth century, and reconstructed many times since then with a view to those wealthy clients who came in season and out.

It was half-past one, time for lunch. Curran walked up the handsome staircase, tired and plodding, to the first floor and the dining-room. He stood in the door-way for an instant, looking round.

A waiter came forward with a dazzle of black and white, the black being his trousers and hair, the white being his coat, his teeth, and a napkin folded upon his wrist. Curran carelessly indicated a free table which stood by a far window in the mild sunlight.

The adjoining table, on his left, stood in a corner where

the daylight did not fully penetrate. The dim wall-light sent enough rose-coloured illumination over the table for the couple who sat there to eat by and the waiter to serve by.

Curran looked in their direction, caught Mary Tiller's eye, and nodded his recognition. She said to her companion, 'There's the gentleman of this morning!' Arnold Leaver turned his head towards Curran, and said, 'Oh, yes, good afternoon. Are you staying here, then?'

'We moved from that Pensione,' said Mary Tiller.

Arnold made a small little laugh. 'My son didn't seem to approve of Mrs Tiller,' he said.

'Oh, well,' she said, 'it wasn't so much the young man, but the whole place, too. Not very relaxing. After all that, I had unpacked my things, we went out for a walk and we looked round. I didn't know there would be a very good hotel like this open at this time of year, but to our amazement we came across the Lord Byron. So we decided there and then to move.'

'Personally,' said Curran, 'I think the Pensione Sofia has a charm of its own—'

'Oh, certainly,' said Mary, 'all its own.'

'It's just that we felt a bit squashed-in with my son Robert snooping round,' said Arnold.

The waiter brought their first course, a complicated creamy pasta-dish dotted with some bright green herbs. Mary studied this intently for a moment, then raised it to her nose to sniff at it. She put down the plate and looked afar off, savouring and analysing the smell.

Arnold laughed, more at ease. He turned to Curran, indicating his companion, and said, 'She's a cooking expert – very hard to please.'

Curran smiled benignly from his table, and with a slightly dismissive gesture turned to the menu-card that the waiter had put in his hand. The couple at the next table started to prod what had been set before them with their forks.

A carafe of white wine was placed on Curran's table. He gave his order quietly to the waiter who poured some wine, meantime, in Curran's glass. Curran sipped his wine but the couple at the next table were not disposed to leave him alone.

'You know Robert well?' said Arnold, between mouthfuls of his stabbed pasta.

'Quite well. I live in Paris.'

'Are you an art historian?' Arnold said.

'You could put it that way,' said Curran with a modest smile that conveyed a certain understatement on Arnold's part. Curran lowered his lids while the waiter bent over him to place a plate of smoked ham in front of him. His self-effacing interest in the ham suggested strongly that Arnold should have known, if he had been sufficiently well informed, that Curran was something more than a simple art historian, that he dealt in art collections on a grand scale, was a name.

'You're an artist?' said Mary, quickly.

'I paint,' Curran said, with an air to the effect that there was more to it than that.

Arnold looked as if he had made a gaffe, and Mary did not help the moment to an easy transition to better moments when she said, 'Their *farfarlone al burro con erbe* are not made *ai denti*, which means hard, and by Anglo-Saxon standards, undercooked. They should be hard. The pasta is overcooked for the tourist trade I imagine. It's too soft. I expect they think it's what we want.'

'Of course,' Curran said, eating his ham. 'I quite agree.' He buttered a thin piece of toast which lay cuddling its fellows in the folds of a napkin.

'I'm glad to hear that Robert is—' Arnold said; but again Mary butted in. She said, with her openly impudent smile which could be on some occasions so charming, 'Do you know, Mr Curran, when we met you this morning with Robert I was convinced you were a private detective. And now we meet you again here. You wouldn't be a private detective by any chance? I mean, sent to watch us?'

'Mary dear!' said her friend.

Curran smiled across the table to her with friendly indulgence.

'No, I'm not,' he said. 'What an exciting idea, though. One wouldn't feel guilty about snooping if one were sent to snoop.'

'Do you feel guilty, Mr Curran?'

'Not a bit,' Curran said.

'Mary!' said Arnold. But he smiled; and to Curran he looked, then, every inch a headmaster.

Curran said, 'I never feel guilty. Even when I should.'

'I always feel guilty,' Mary said. 'I love it. I don't really feel alive without a feeling of guilt.'

Arnold apparently wanted to concentrate on eating. Mary

looked at her companion; she seemed to adore him, although from an objective point of view he didn't seem particularly adorable, that was all.

While waiting for his second course Arnold Leaver gave his childish laugh and said to Curran, 'Any idea what Robert is doing here in Venice?'

'How like Robert you look just now!' Curran said.

Arnold looked perplexed. Curran said: 'Your son is doing research, so far as I understand.'

'You came here with him?' Arnold said.

'No, he'd already transferred to Venice when I bumped into him,' Curran said.

'What brings him to Venice? He didn't write home that he was going to Venice.'

'Young men seldom tell their parents of their plans.'

'Venice,' said Robert's father, while a fleck of the Venetian sunlight caught his small yellow moustache. 'What is he studying in Venice? In Paris, he—'

'There might be a girl behind it, who knows?' said Curran.

Mary said, chirpily, 'That's what I've been thinking.'

Arnold said, 'A *what*?'

'A girl,' said Curran, coolly.

'Oh, yes,' Arnold said, looking hard at the salad that had been placed at the side of his main dish. He was embarrassed, now, at having revealed surprise. Mary was tasting a piece of veal done in white-wine sauce, her eyes fixed on the far distance while she related the sensation of her taste-buds to her always better judgment. Having swallowed the test-piece she narrowed her eyes analytically, moving her tongue inside her mouth. 'Well, Arnold,' she said, 'isn't that nice that he has a girl? You know, you always misjudge that boy.'

'Oh, come, it isn't a question of judging, misjudging. No, I don't stand judgment on anybody, far less Robert. He has his own life to live. Goodness me!' Again, the childish laugh, the laugh of one who had been too long a schoolmaster, life-steeped in the job. 'Mary,' he informed Curran, 'is a professional cook, that's why she's so interested in the preparation of her food.'

Mary was ruminating over her salad. 'I enjoyed that veal dish,' she declared, 'with every fibre of my being. How about you, dear?'

'Very good,' he said.

'Mrs Tiller, are you food-tasting for a travel book or something?' Curran said.

'Not just at the moment,' she said. 'But I'm always tempted to take on a job like that. I always remember a restaurant, how the food is prepared, what it's like, how it's served. It all goes down firmly in my memory.'

'Mary taught cooking at a boys' school where I was headmaster,' Arnold said.

'A boys' school!' Curran marvelled.

'Oh, the classes were a great success. More and more men have to cook their own food and like it,' Arnold said, and Mary added, 'The boys had to eat what they cooked, so they soon learned the rudiments.'

'After all,' said Arnold, as if arguing with a parent, 'cookery is chemistry.'

Curran paid his bill and left the couple discussing the

cheese to follow. When they said goodbye they asked him, in unison, to come to drinks one evening; this was obviously a decision they had made together in a quiet exchange in the course of the meal, probably while the waiter was attending to them, or to Curran, with a clatter of serving-spoons. Curran consulted his diary and accepted with thanks, casually, as if inattentive to the unknown contingencies of anything to come.

Mary waved her hand. 'About seven tomorrow evening in the bar,' she said.

About seven next evening Curran came down to the lobby of the Hotel Lord Byron and settled in a chair in the bar-parlour beside Mary Tiller and Arnold Leaver who were waiting for him.

Mary was wearing a fur stole round her shoulders although the hotel was centrally heated. She had that outstanding look she had the first time he had seen her on her arrival at the Pensione Sofia.

She said, 'It's cosier in our room. We have a refrigerator and plenty of drinks up there.'

'Yes, let's go upstairs,' Arnold said.

The room was large with some comfortable chairs besides a huge ornamental bed; this bed was shaped like a swan, with gilded black swans' heads forming the foot-posts. At the top of the bed two swans, quilted in body, met face to face with black lacquered heads and golden eyes and beaks. The ceiling was painted in a bright blue and white skyscape. Across this several cherubs blew puffily at a white-grey prancing horse and a very flesh-coloured nude classical rider whose biceps were so large as to be not really healthy.

'It's not fake,' Arnold Leaver said, indicating these splendours. 'The ceiling's eighteenth century, restored of course, but original.'

Curran said he could well believe it. His own room, he said, was in the modern wing.

'Don't you like Venetian styles?' Mary said.

Curran said he didn't think the eighteenth century was their best period.

'Well, that's a fair observation,' Arnold said, as if making a note on an exam paper.

'I can't tell you what fun it is,' said Mary Tiller, 'occupying a room like this. It's fun. Especially as we're on a fun-trip, you know, Arnold and I. They call this the honeymoon room, of course.'

The abundant array of beauty bottles and jars on the dressing-table seemed to fit these grim words. Moisture cream, day nourishing cream, night cream, muscle oil – there must have been more than twenty bottles to bring aid and comfort to the fun-trip. Mary glanced in the direction of the dressing-table as Curran did, the sad mirror sizing her up before she looked away again.

'What will you drink? Whisky?' Arnold said.

'Very good,' said Curran. 'That's my drink.'

Mary sat swirling her glass so that the ice in it rattled. Arnold, on his way to the bathroom to refill the ice-tray, said, 'It's been a fine day, cold of course, but we didn't stay in. Mary and I—' he reappeared with the watery ice-tray carefully balanced, and continued as he edged it into the freezer of the small refrigerator, '—we went out, all the same. We went to the Frari church to see *The Assumption* of Titian. Marvellous!' He sat down and took up his gin and tonic.

'What an experience!' Mary said.

Arnold said, 'Mr Curran, I want to tell you something about my wife.'

'Why me?' said Curran.

'Mr Curran, we want to talk to you,' Mary said.

'Just call me plain Curran,' Curran said. 'That goes for first name and second name with my friends.'

'Curran. That's nice,' Mary said.

'We decided, Mary and I,' said Arnold, 'that we should open up a bit to you. We decided today, while we were on our rounds of the churches, that we should take you into confidence. After all, you're my son's friend and, no doubt, adviser.'

Curran smiled, feeling wary, hoping they were not going to pump him about Robert but, rather, let themselves be pumped. 'I'm hardly Robert's Father-confessor,' he said.

'Has he left Venice?' said Mary.

'I really don't know,' Curran said.

'We thought you were both here in Venice together,' she said, glancing at Arnold.

'Well, didn't I tell you we met by chance? One always seems to bump into a friend in Venice, no matter what time of year.'

'Well then, if you're not in Venice as a friend of Robert's what are you here for?' she said.

'Mary!' said Arnold.

'What's the matter?'

'You simply mustn't ask questions like that.'

Curran looked very amused. 'How long have you been on holiday together?' he said.

Mary giggled. Then she said, 'Nearly two weeks. Arnold feels we've been followed. We were in France, you know, and a night in Paris; then Arnold called his wife, who seemed upset, but really, Mr Curran, I mean Curran—'

'I want very much to tell you about my wife Anthea,' Arnold said.

'You seem to trust my discretion,' Curran said. 'But you know, your private affairs are no business of mine.'

'My wife Anthea . . .' Arnold kept on saying as if he had other wives by other names. He leaned back his head as he spoke, his eyes on the horse and rider rearing above him. As Arnold spoke, Curran took the opportunity to stare deliberately at Mary and, having obtained her prompt attention, he slowly winked one eye. She seemed delighted, hunching her shoulders in a quick gesture and puckering her face in a smile of conspiracy.

'My wife Anthea, as I say, is a sensitive, a very sensitive woman. I have tried to give her affection, understanding . . . She had a nervous breakdown three years ago. What is a man to do? A strong, normal man with a big responsibility, running a school, pleasing the Board of Governors, getting a high quota of boys through the university exams, getting the right teachers, controlling them, making the school pay. And all the rest of it—'

'Etcetera, etcetera,' suggested Curran with some nods of comprehension.

'Exactly,' said Arnold. He looked at Mary with a worried, rather sad, smile. 'Then two years ago, exactly, this month, Mary came into the school and into my life. How are your drinks getting on? Mary?'

'I'll help myself,' Mary said. 'Same for you, Curran?'

'Yes, please, Mrs Tiller.'

'Mary, to you,' she said.

'Mary to me,' he said.

'Now, Curran,' said Arnold, 'you, as my son's friend, might know if Robert has, or, on the other hand, if he has not, telephoned, written, telegraphed, or by other method communicated to his mother, that is, my wife Anthea, that my trip to the Continent with Mary is on a basis of close familiarity rather than platonic companionship.'

'Oh, God!' said Curran.

'Oh God what?' said Arnold.

Mary said, 'I think our friend doesn't want to answer these questions.'

Curran said, 'Not when they're put in that way. Anyhow, I don't know anything about Robert's personal affairs, but I think it very unlikely he should bother his mother with distressing information.'

'He's capable of anything,' Arnold said.

'Do you know,' Curran said, 'I think you're imagining a lot of things.'

Mary said, 'Well, we know, or at least guess to the point of certainty, that you're Anthea's private detective.' She smiled intimately at Curran. He smiled back responsively. 'Not at all,' he said, without emphasis.

Arnold apparently had taken a few drinks before Curran's arrival, for he was now getting on for drunk. He got up, slightly staggered, made his way towards the table where the bottles and glasses were set out, and started to refill his glass, his eyes glaring at it as if it had outraged him in some way. Mary came to his rescue, so that the glass brimmed over a little less than it would otherwise have done.

Curran looked at his watch and got up while he said he was afraid he must go.

Arnold looked at him with the same outraged stare, and was about to make another speech when Curran rapidly said goodnight.

Mary came out with him. The lift was near their room.

Curran looked at her merrily. 'He never got round to telling me about his wife Anthea.'

'He's brooding over it,' she said. 'Sometimes he can be very happy when he's had a drop too much. But not when he's brooding on Anthea.'

'Well, goodnight.'

She said, 'Call me at nine tomorrow morning. He goes down to breakfast but I always have mine in bed at that hour.'

Curran turned back to the room and, looking in, saw Arnold still standing uncertainly at the foot of the atrocious bed.

'Would it help you if I took Mary off your hands for a while?' Curran said.

'What!'

'She's a very attractive woman,' Curran said.

Mary said, from behind Curran, 'Arnold, he's joking.'

'Get out!' Arnold said.

Curran went back to the lift. 'That might take his mind off his wife Anthea,' he said to Mary.

3

Outside it was beautifully sunny weather in a rare, golden October. It is one of the secrets of Nature in its mood of mockery that fine weather lays a heavier weight on the minds and hearts of the depressed and the inwardly tormented than does a really bad day with dark rain snivelling continuously and sympathetically from a dirty sky:

> Come autumn sae pensive, in yellow and grey,
> And soothe me wi' tidings o' nature's decay;
> The dark, dreary winter, and wild-driving snaw,
> Alane can delight me – now Nannie's awa.

Into the glorious street of a Birmingham suburb stepped Anthea Leaver click-clacking her heels so sharply on the pavement that nobody who walked in front of her failed to hear her coming, and make way for her, since she was walking faster than anybody else.

Her destination, however, was merely the bus-stop where she had to wait like everybody else. The people in front of her in the queue now pulled themselves straight and slouched no more as if anxious not to further provoke the terrorist who had clicked into position in her tweed coat, stick-like, wearing tinted glasses. Others dribbled into line behind Anthea in various attitudes of slouch, clearly unaware of her from the start; a young couple with two children, then the bus.

Anthea got on the bus as if she meant business and got off two stops later, from where she clicked smartly across the road to the garage. There the car, fresh from a wash, polish and overhaul, was waiting for her. She paid sternly, folded up her receipt with precision and put it away in her bag. Then she drove off to Coventry, to the private investigation agency where she had an appointment. She stopped once before she got there on the very outskirts of Coventry to park the car. There were a few golden trees and the leaves lay on the pavement as if Coventry were pastoral as of old. Then she took a taxi to her destination.

The offices of GESS (Global-Equip Security Services) Ltd were one floor up a narrow stair in a run-down side-street, so that it was inside the main entrance door that the difference abruptly emphasized itself. The offices had an established legal atmosphere in that there was a lot of wood prematurely aged for the purpose on the walls of the interior. The entrance hall was lined with this dark wood, with bare wooden floors, highly polished. Anthea was asked to take a seat by the receptionist, who then explained, 'Mr B. is on the

phone.' Anthea seemed to try not to look at the receptionist; she seemed embarrassed to be there, as if the place was a
pawnshop or a Roman Catholic confessional which one
might be seen going into or coming out of. A folded brochure
lay on the table beside her. Somebody had left it open, or perhaps it had been deliberately placed in a certain position for
clients like her. Anthea could read without moving her head
one of the columns suggesting, in an inscrutable order of
syntax, what GESS could offer, discover, cure . . .

Missing persons
Backgrounds checked
Polygraph (Lie Detector) Examinations
Complete Crime Laboratory
Uniformed • Armed Guards • Plain-clothes • Negligence
Motion pictures
Matrimonial Escorts
Latest modern Equip
Apprehensions and Tailing
Fidelity Department
Skip Tracing
Construction and Plant Protection
Prompt • Precise • Discreet
Bureau of Ethics and Charisma
Male, female operators

Anthea looked back up the list and stopped at 'Fidelity
Department'. That must be me, she thought, and looked up
to find the receptionist staring at her. 'Mr B. is still on the

phone to Brussels,' said the girl. 'But you're a few minutes early, anyway.'

Anthea looked at her watch and then said, 'What is the gentleman's name did you say?'

'The clients use only the initial of our executives. Your executive is Mr B.'

'Mr B.,' Anthea repeated.

'Security,' said the girl as if it were a sad, well-worn response in the litany of her working days. Her hand went to the box in front of her. There was a click. She then droned to Anthea, 'Mr B. is free now. Will you come this way?'

Mr B. not only smiled as Anthea entered his office, but in a sense continued to smile. Even when he got up, took her hand, and said, 'Mrs Leaver. I've been expecting you,' he had that extraordinary expression, so that it looked as if he had been smiling and waiting for her a long lifetime.

She sat in the chair he had waved her into. It was not quite a smile that he gave but a shape of mouth and lips that he had been born with, a wide, fat-lipped mouth. Behind his glasses his eyes were not smiling; they were abstractly looking at the situation in hand, his client. He was fair, robust, in his early thirties. Who would have known but that his mouth-smile with the fruity closed lips might have got him into trouble in a court of law, before a judge and jury, should he have been giving evidence in a desperately serious case. His desk was clear of papers. He took from a side-drawer of the desk a foolscap-sized, photo-copied form and laid it in front of him.

'Now, then.' He took up the desk-pen. 'Full name and address, telephone . . .'

Her determination and her storm-trooper attitude had not lasted but Anthea was sufficiently in possession of herself to say, when Mr B. came to ask her to sign the form, 'Before I do that, we must discuss the price. I must know the price. It's possible I can't afford your services.'

He put aside the form and brought out of the front drawer of his desk, tilting backward in the process, a stack of small oblong folded cards. They were unused, and in style similar to place-cards set out on the table at large and formal dinner-parties, with the names of the guests. Mr B. silently made a row of three cards on the desk in front of him, and behind them a further row of six. He had set about making yet a third row when he spoke. 'The price,' he said, 'depends entirely on what you want, where you want it done, and how long the service will take. You must first give me some rough details before we can discuss the fee'; and as he spoke the word 'rough' he seemed to smile more than nature had predestined him to do.

'Oh, well,' said Anthea, 'I didn't want to waste your time, that's all. I just want you to know right from the start that I don't own a fleet of yachts and I haven't got big money, diamonds ...'

'GESS is here to help you,' said Mr B. 'Let's leave the Rolls-Royces out of it and not delude ourselves. Would it be a matrimonial difficulty?'

Anthea agreed that it was that kind of question. He wrote something on one of the little cards and set it in another place on the desk. 'Tell me the whole story,' he said. She went on with the whole story for about twenty minutes during which time he smilingly lifted the cards, one by one, to make notes on them. The first time he did this she halted; but he said, 'Don't mind me. Carry on.'

She might have been lying on a couch, and he taking notes where she couldn't see him. She looked at him with disapproval as much as to say some of his questions were precocious at this first meeting.

'Are you in love with your husband?'

'I don't think that has anything to do with any arrangement we may come to.'

'It's only that we do try to discourage clients from embarking on an investigative venture if, in fact, they have no significant final interest in the pursuit.'

'I asked you to name the price,' she said.

'I can't possibly tell you yet,' said smiling Mr B. 'But your husband having gone abroad with this other lady, well, bang goes a pretty penny to start with. We have to send a man abroad to consult with our expert on the spot, and we need to have local informers, very expensive and somewhat – shall I say? – a local hazard in the area concerned. We have no territorial rights. Expenses here, expenses there, they mount up.'

His cards were all over the clear table like a regatta assembling on a calm bay, outside which the infinite sea chopped everywhere.

He smiled a real smile, which was not much different from the normal. 'Mrs Leaver,' he said, 'we haven't yet got all our cards on the table, have we?'

She didn't smile back.

'Or haven't we? I want to find out, you see, if it's worth your money investigating your husband's activities in Venice. Do you really care?'

'Of course I do,' she said.

'You're still in love with him?'

'That's not the point,' she said. 'He's my husband.'

'A possible divorce? Alimony?' he said. 'We are counsellors, you know, counsellors. Do you depend on him entirely, financially?'

She said nothing for a while, only watching him distrustfully. Then as if by a stroke of lucid madness she nevertheless went on eagerly, 'He holds most of the property and his lady-friend is supposed to be rich.'

He made notes on two cards, smiling, perhaps as if thinking: She says he has most of the property but it could be the other way round. Or perhaps he was only smiling because he couldn't help it. He said, 'Lady-friend supposed to be rich.'

'I don't care how rich she is or attractive,' Anthea said, speaking rapidly. 'I just want to know what my husband's up to. He's my husband. I want to know. Do you understand? I believe in one man, one vote.'

'You mean one man, one woman,' he said.

'Yes, that's what I said.'

'No, you said one man, one vote.'

'Nothing of the sort. What has the vote got to do with it? You must have misheard.'

'All right. Now, if you don't mind my asking, Mrs Leaver, what did you marry him for in the first place? Do you recall?

Was it infatuation, love, or let's say security if he has a house and money, or a mixture of factors ...'

She looked alert when he said, 'house and money', as if some suspicion held her. She leaned forward and said to him with some earnestness, 'I've often thought over why I married my husband. I have concluded that I married for marriage in general, but more specifically for my wedding day, the event, the white dress, the hymns and the flowers, the picture in the papers. However, that doesn't concern you.'

'Your picture in the papers,' he said.

'I am not a criminal,' said Anthea as if forcing him to mean that she was.

'Good gracious, no. Has he suggested a parting?'

'No, oh, no. He's too comfortable with me.'

Mr B. made some notes on the two latest of the small folded cards and stood them in position for the boat-race.

'Venice!' she said. 'It's an insult taking another person to Venice, and never me. We had our honeymoon on the Isle of Wight, but that was back in the humble days. Now it's Venice. And my son is in Paris at the university studying art history. Everyone abroad, except me. No wonder people ask me, where is my sense of humour?'

Mr B. picked up another card. 'How many children?'

'Only one. A son. I want to keep him out of it. He doesn't count. Don't make any card for him, please.'

'Well, his name and age. It's only that ...'

She shouted, 'My son doesn't exist as far as you're concerned. He's out of it, right out of it. I shouldn't have mentioned him.'

'Well, now, the minimum preliminary costs ... Let me see ...' Mr B. shifted the cards, re-reading each one carefully. 'Only an approximation, of course, because we may have to have other meetings, Mrs Leaver, after the data is processed. It has to be processed. The reason for these separate cards is, let me tell you, for your own protection. They are so distributed in our processing system as to defeat any attempt to steal the said information. Nobody would know where to look. The data are in several places at once. – Something like ourselves, if I may say so.' He laughed on top of his smile, then added, 'Only we, very few of us, would know the complete picture, you can rest assured of that.'

'The price?' Anthea said. 'If it runs to hundreds and thousands, I'm afraid—'

'Don't be afraid,' said Mr B. 'Above all, avoid being afraid.'

Anthea fumbled in her bag and made visible the tip of a leather-encased cheque-book.

'No, no,' said Mr B. His hand came out across the desk to arrest her action. 'We don't do business like that,' he said.

'Anything I can possibly afford,' she said. 'I only want to know. It's worth any price I can possibly pay.'

'Mrs Leaver,' he said, 'each case is different from another.' He looked at his little armada of cards. 'I have decided,' he said, 'that your case is different. It is utterly unique. First let us get some results for you and then we can see what we can afford to pay, shall we? Perhaps we won't have anything to pay.' He gave a smile on top of his fixed one. 'You're a very charming person, Mrs Leaver. I hope that money will not come into our relationship – at least, not to any appreciable extent.'

He then coped, in comfortable words, with her confused amazement and got up to usher her out.

'We'll be in touch with you as soon as we have processed the cards. We may even have something concrete,' he said as she left the office. 'But if you need counsel at any time be sure to refer to me, Mr B. of Global-Equip Security Services, Mr B. of GESS. Do not, for your own sake, I emphasize, for your own sake, attempt any investigations on your own account. Leave it to us. Leave it to GESS.' He opened the door of his office to let her pass through. 'Mr B., Global-Equip,' he said.

She looked at him before she walked out and said, 'Human nature is evil, isn't it?'

His features did not change, nor his smiling lips open, but he made a small cynical snort. Then he said, 'I wouldn't call it evil. Human nature is human nature as far as I'm concerned.'

Grace, who in other words was Mrs N. Gregory, was waiting on the doorstep, her upbraiding bosom in semi-profile, when Anthea got home. 'Oh, God, Grace,' Anthea said, 'I forgot you were coming.'

'I've been and come, been and come again,' Grace said. 'I thought something must have happened to you. I thought, if nothing's happened and she's only forgotten, then I'll soon tell her her fortune.'

She stumped into the house after Anthea. 'Grace,' said Anthea. 'Wait till you hear what's happened. No wonder I forgot you were coming. I've taken steps.'

*

The Leavers had occupied this house, where Grace and Anthea sat talking, since the previous July. Before that, their residence for eighteen years had been an old rectory in the grounds of Ambrose College, the boys' school where the absent Arnold Leaver had been headmaster.

'God and public opinion will judge,' Anthea said, as if the two were one and the same. She and Grace Gregory sipped their sherry.

Arnold's retirement and the move to a better-equipped but less imposing house had upset Arnold to the extent that as soon as his books were finally in place on the new shelves he declared himself exhausted in body and mind. He returned from his doctor with an 'order' that he should take a holiday, with a 'strong recommendation' that he should go without his wife. It was early in October.

Anthea made a furious telephone call to Arnold's doctor but got no farther than the snooty receptionist who told her the doctor would not discuss his patients except with their consent and in their presence. Anthea threatened to sue the doctor for disruption of family life, and in this way got the last word; but that only, she being too angry, inarticulate, dismayed and outraged to pin herself down to finding a lawyer at that moment. Arnold left the next week for the Continent, quite calmly.

Anthea telephoned around to her friends invoking God and public opinion on her side. She found a lawyer who told her that what Arnold had done was perfectly reasonable, and within his rights. A holiday abroad on his own. But, said frantic Anthea, he isn't on his own. He has a travelling companion, a rich lady, and he says it's platonic. That's something else again, said the lawyer. Perhaps he's going through a phase. The lawyer's desk was covered with papers and files. He looked bored. At the end of that week Anthea had made up her mind and had gone to GESS of Coventry.

Grace Gregory had been Matron at Ambrose College up till a few months ago when she retired. She had taken with her into retirement a boy, now eighteen, who had spent his schooldays at Ambrose College. He was lodging with her while working at his first job in a travel agency, being good at languages.

'I mustn't stay, or my young lodger Leo won't have his supper,' said Grace.

'I've got to talk to someone,' Anthea said. 'Can't you ring him up and say you'll be late?'

'He gives me such laundry problems,' Grace said. 'And you should see him eat. Just the same as when he was at school. But never mind; I like Leo, he's good company, that boy. He thinks the world of me. Have you heard from his Nibs in Venice?'

'He phoned from Paris on his way to Venice. Sounded guilty, really guilty. I said, "Is your woman there with you?" He said, "You mean my colleague?" I said, "I mean your woman." He said, "You must be referring to my platonic friend." So, Grace, you'll never believe. I've been to a private investigation concern and placed the matter in their hands.'

'You must have more money than sense,' Grace said.

'I haven't paid anything. They're going ahead without any deposit. I told the man everything – at least, as much as he needed to know. He seemed to be quite on my side.'

'Someone will have to pay,' said Grace, nodding wisely into the second fold of her neck. 'If you get in the hands of a private eye someone's got to pay through the nose.' She wagged her forefinger and tapped her toe, pressing as many images of physiognomy into the scene as might bring reality Anthea's way. 'Why didn't you come to me?' she said. 'I wasn't Matron at Ambrose College for eighteen years without learning something about private investigation.'

'Oh, no, Grace,' Anthea said. 'This has got to be done objectively by a firm of experts. I made up my mind and I did it. The person I saw was very understanding towards me, and very efficient. I had cold shivers at first but he grew on me, and I've promised to wait till he gets in touch with me.'

Grace mused, as she gathered up her shopping-bag and gloves and umbrella, 'Nosey Parkers never hear any good of themselves.'

'I only want the truth,' said Anthea.

'All this fuss,' said Grace. 'What's marriage these days? It's only a bit of paper. I've got to get back to Leo; he's a hungry lad and if I'm not there to get his supper he sits around like a spray of deadly nightshade waiting for someone to pick it.'

Anthea watched the news on two channels while she ate her supper. Then she took up her library book, a novel comfortingly like the last novel she had read:

Matt and Joyce finished their supper in semi-silence. Somehow she couldn't bring herself to ask the vital question: had he got the job? Was it so vital, was anything so vital anyway?

If he had got the job he would have said so without her asking.

Matt got up and stacked the dishes. She followed him into the kitchen and ran the hot tap. What had there ever been between them? Had it all been an illusion? The rain poured outside. Mamie's knickers and two of John's pullovers were drying in the kitchen. She looked at the damp clothes and found no significance in them. Matt looked at the kitchen clock. 'Half-past ten. I must have been late!' he exclaimed.

'You were late,' she remarked, slipping the dishes into the drying-rack.

Matt stood, unmoving.

'Colin and Beryl rang,' she sighed.

Anthea's eyes drooped. And so to bed.

4

'I just told him,' Robert said, 'to go to hell.'

'You shouldn't have done that,' Lina said. 'That man is very important. Maybe he could get me a job. Perhaps he could help to find my father's grave. You should ask him to accompany us to the cemetery—'

'Oh, as to your father's grave, he knows one thing about that – he isn't buried at San Michele. Curran might even have an idea where he's buried. "Victor Pancev," he said. He seems to have known your father away back in history.'

'I have to meet with Curran,' she said.

'Oh, that won't be necessary.'

'I would like to ask him some questions.'

'Curran,' said Robert, 'asks the questions, generally speaking. Or, to put it more precisely, he demands to know. All very politely, of course. Curran is a cultivated man.'

'Could he get me a job?'

'He could command you a job. Curran would believe he was God if he believed in God. All his life Curran has commanded the morning and caused the dayspring to know its place.'

'It sounds crazy,' she said. 'Why do you boast about Curran to me? Do you boast about me to Curran?'

'Yes, because you're my first girl, and he knows it. And I told him to go to hell.'

'Then why are you frightened?'

'I'm not afraid of Curran.'

'You're afraid of something.'

'He says you're being followed,' Robert said. 'And that it's dangerous for me to be seen with you.'

'Being followed? Let them follow. I have asylum. I have residential rights, and my father's grave is here in Venice. I will go to the police and complain. And I have to get a job because my refugee fund money isn't enough. And nobody wants my paintings in Venice. I'm a defector and I have my rights. Maybe I get a job in a movie.'

She walked around her little room, agitated but inhibited by the cramped space and the physical obstacles in the way of every step, the surfaces of which were moreover covered entirely by food-tins, paint-tins, crockery, her drawing-boards and her crayons, her bag of flour, her jar of salt, her folded clothes piled high, and Robert himself sprawling in the chair.

But Robert wasn't listening to her anyway. He was wondering whether to tell her, too, to go to hell, this being his mood of that day. He saw, from the washing-line extending from Lina's little window, her green bulbous drawers hung out to dry; sometimes, so she told him, she found this garment useful for shoplifting in the grocery departments, when her cheque from the refugee fund in Paris was late in arriving, or when she ran out of money at the end of the month.

He said, 'Maybe you'd like to meet my father, too. He's turned up in Venice with his mistress.'

'With his mistress, are you saying?'

'That's right.'

She was very shocked. There was no knowing what would shock Lina.

'Why do they come to Venice when you come to Venice? It's you that's being followed, not me.'

'Everyone,' said Robert, 'comes to Venice. Yourself, for example—'

'But he has no right to bring his mistress to you.'

'He brought her to Venice, not to me,' Robert said.

'Who is she? What a woman! How could she come to Venice? Is she a Jew?' Lina had a stubborn phobia about Jews, a burden of her upbringing which had lost her most of her friends in Paris. On learning that Mary was not a Jew, so far as Robert was aware, Lina next enquired as to Mary's profession.

'She's a cookery teacher, but that's only a hobby. She's rich. I rather liked the look of her,' Robert said. 'She was showy and flashy which I think is right for a mistress.'

Lina started to cry. She said, 'I don't understand half the words you say, and now you want another woman, you have desire.'

Robert repeated in French, which she could better follow,

all he had said and more; he spoke quite slowly with a venom that had no bearing on the present occasion; except that, feeling in a bad mood, he saw no need whatsoever to control it.

Lina said, 'I will meet with your father. I will meet with Curran. I will tell them the story how I got away for a better life. It's a great story.' She was crying even more, as she worked herself up with the drama of her story.

Robert started to feel enjoyment, and laughed.

Lina Pancev, now aged thirty-five, had grown up in post-war Bulgaria. Her father had disappeared the year she was born, while Bulgaria was still under German occupation. Victor Pancev had been a minor official at the court of King Boris of Bulgaria; the king was a fairly silly man who had playmates rather than friends; Victor Pancev was one of these. The king collapsed and died one day, poisoned, it was said, at the instigation of the Germans. Victor Pancev disappeared on the day of the funeral, never to return. Some weeks later his wife, in Bulgaria, had a letter from a friend who had seen him in Venice where he was staying with a Bulgarian count at a house called Villa Sofia. She had a postcard from Victor himself, not in his usual style, to say he was well and busy. Shortly after this, Lina was born.

Amid the chaos of war, when Russian liberators in Bulgaria followed upon German liberators, and in Italy the Allies finally liberated right, left and centre, the noble owner of the Villa Sofia in Venice died a natural death, while his friend Victor Pancev was killed. This was all that could ever be ascertained afterwards by his friends. Who killed him and why, nobody knew. It was said that he was killed by monarchist agents of Bulgaria who suspected him of having been part of the plot to poison King Boris. But the two maidservants who remained in the Villa testified only that he was found dead in the garden and that his body was 'taken away'.

The two servants were Katerina and Eufemia. They inherited the Villa under the will of the old count, who had no relatives at his death; it was supposed they were his illegitimate daughters.

Lina Pancev grew up in communist Bulgaria in the midst of a large family of cousins, uncles, aunts, and step-brothers, for as soon as Victor Pancev's death was officially established his widow had married again.

Lina had no interest in the past, King Boris and all that set about whom her elders sometimes let fall nostalgic phrases, even sentences. She had an early talent for drawing; later she learned to paint objects with photographic exactitude, and to portray people a little larger than life. She did views of monasteries, hills and landscapes, cloudscapes, flowers on a table; she went to the Black Sea and did work-groups at the docks all looking in the same direction, very tanned; and she excelled at women, large and strong, coming out of a shoe factory near her home, all looking healthy and refreshed after a good day's work. These women were in some demand from Lina's hand. It might have been, when she finished her studies in applied architecture at the university, that she could have been able to earn her living by her paintings alone.

One summer, her second cousin and boy-friend, Serge,

returned from London, having spent six months there on a student exchange programme. Lina sat by the open window, doing nothing, with the flower-boxes of pink geraniums on the sill beside her, listening to Serge as he talked during the long summer evening. He was lean-faced, tall and idealistic, with vivid large brown eyes and a dark skin.

Lina's mother came in with a bowl of fruit, jaunty, still with her slim figure, her hair smartly cut, her dimples and pointed chin. She laughed as Serge, without waiting for the knife and the fruit-plate to come, took a peach and bit right into it with his white teeth. Lina laughed, too. The mother left the room and Serge continued to talk against the noise of traffic and children in the street below.

He spoke in the manner of his own education; automatically he exaggerated, and he meant it. England, he said, was full of ideological contradictions. They were hypocrites, especially the young people; their left-wing movement was a laugh. Nice people sometimes, but only because of their innocence; they simply did not know themselves, and how truly they were bloated capitalists. Three meals a day, and always money in their pockets; you couldn't distinguish between them and the Americans.

Most of all Serge talked about the woman in Hampstead he had stayed with for a while; it was a love-affair 'at least if you call it a love-affair when there's no illusion of permanency on either side'.

Lina prepared a supper of ham omelettes; she laid two places, for they were alone in the house, her step-brothers and sisters being either in the country with relatives or at a youth camp, and her mother gone off to play cards, her step-father working late in the shipping office where he was a manager, international section. Lina told Serge to stop eating the fruit lest he spoil his appetite, and to save up his story while she went to prepare the supper. She felt the woman in Hampstead was the part of his tale she was hungry for, like supper. Swiftly she cut the bread and bore it in with the omelettes, all on one tray, with the tomato and cucumber salad.

'Well, what about her, your London woman?' she said after they had started to eat. Serge, encouraged by the success of his general report, had, in Lina's short absence in the kitchen, assembled the next part of his story to mind, in closely remembered detail which he arranged for the best possible effect. He wanted simultaneously to make Lina jealous and to impress her with his masculinity in having managed to have a love-affair in the midst of all his busy time in London; and he wanted also to reassure her that the woman, capitalist bourgeoise as she was, left-wing as she claimed to be, was not remotely to be thought of seriously by an intellectual Bulgarian like himself.

'Her name,' said Lina, with an air of first things first.

'Deborah,' he said.

'How old?'

'About thirty-eight, with two children, one ten the other thirteen, both girls, sulky and ugly.'

'Deborah is ugly?'

'Maybe she is now. I haven't seen her for three weeks. She had a tough face and a lanky figure. No make-up and she didn't comb her hair very much, maybe twice a week. Occupation, journalist, very spiteful in her writing. The house was a terrible mess, especially the bedroom. It was a pretty house in itself, very expensive, but Deborah let everything go, maybe years ago, as she let her husband go. She trails around with long skirts and droopy shoulders all day. She drinks and she takes a little drugs. Not much to sleep with, but it was an experience, a love-affair for the time being; you can't get much in London.'

'Rich?' said Lina.

'Oh, yes. Of course she thought she was poor. She always complained about money. But she had money from the husband and maybe that money was really for the children, but she lived off it. When there was someone she didn't like, she would try to make money out of them. It seemed so, all the time. First, the husband, and then when she needed money badly she would write an article against someone in the public eye, attacking them for the best parts of their work, people like sculptors or writers: she would pick out the best of their work and make it out to be the worst, or maybe she would attack a man for his car, or a woman for her clothes, all the time pretending to be the social conscience of her age. The articles made her a lot of money as she told me – she made a private joke of them. Bernard Shaw used to do it, she said, and built up his reputation by attacking the reputations already made. There is no such thing as objective judgment in London. Deborah lives how she likes; she can order in the carpenter to build cupboards in her house whenever she likes; there were eight rooms for three people, herself and the girls.

She called herself left-wing, nearly communist. It's very, very funny, Lina. You have to go there to realize how it is.'

'Why did you go with Deborah if you despised her?'

'I didn't despise her. I just saw she didn't know what she was doing or saying. She was generous, sometimes. I couldn't afford to buy her many presents, only little things like one flower, one dahlia on a stem, which she loved. She let me do some cooking in her kitchen and she bought in the food. Then sometimes we went out for a meal and paid our own share, but sometimes she paid for us both.'

'And the poor daughters?'

'Hateful. Rude and horrible. I think Deborah could see they were terrible and secretly didn't like them, either. She gave them money to go out and eat pizzas or English sandwiches at mealtimes, and they had money for the cinema. It was always money in the hands of those girls, a dreadful upbringing. One of them called me "that bloody Pole" in my own presence. Deborah merely said "Bulgarian", and left it at that.'

Serge went on about Deborah and some of her friends in London, late into the evening. 'Will you write to her?' Lina asked. 'Well, no, I don't think so,' said Serge, 'and yet, maybe later on I'll write a note. It depends how I feel later on. And then, you know, Deborah might be useful.'

'She might be dangerous,' Lina said.

'That's a very bright point. She might indeed. But she's very boring, even to her friends, I could see that.'

'Dangerous people often seem boring,' said Lina.

'So do useful people, very often,' mused Serge.

He did not discern what type of alert interest Lina was taking in his story, his anecdotes of London, of university life, his hosts and hostesses, the Hampstead of Deborah and the Deborah of Hampstead. He understood only that she was entertained by his travellers' tales, and the absurdity of the foreign ways he was describing.

He was unaware that the same story that can repel can also enchant, according to the listener. It happened that Lina's imagination was inflamed with the exciting possibilities of western life, the more Serge reported what he had perceived as hilarious decadence. Taking it for granted she was exactly of his mind, he expounded on the wastefulness, the selfishness, the inequality, the social injustice and the hypocrisy of western left-wing ideas, illustrating them with anecdotes till Lina's mother came home, looked in on them, smiled, said goodnight and went to bed. Even then Serge went on and on, while Lina drank in the marvels, as they appeared to her, of wearing long skirts and tangled hair in an eight-room house, very expensive, with two liberated daughters and a husband who wasn't there but who paid the bills. She was stirred by the sheer magic of being a woman with enough money to take a handsome Polish or Bulgarian student out to dine at a restaurant and home to bed. Lina, who was then twenty-three, transformed in her mind as she listened, even the farthest peripheries of Serge's account. ' . . . She was arranging flowers in the sitting-room. She had only just got home from the office, her car was still outside the gate. There was a ring at the bell; she opened the door; it was a man who said he was the piano-tuner for the people upstairs who had a flat there – you see it was a divided house. Well, she let him go up, without thinking any more about it, and do you know, he was a big-time thief, he took all their ...' To Lina, the magic ideas were contained in the phrases, 'just got home from the office ... her car outside the gate'; ' ... piano-tuner for the people upstairs ...'; ' ... she was arranging flowers in the sitting-room'; and it didn't signify in the least to Lina that the story was about a big-time thief, so long as these phrases were dancing in her ears, making colours in the mind's eye.

It was rather like the time, only a few years ago, when a tourist-lady from Moscow had called with a letter of introduction to Lina's mother in Sofia. The stranger had reminisced a while, talking wistfully about the years before the war, the late nineteen thirties, in the same way as the old White Russians were said to speak of the years before the revolution. The woman tourist's husband had evidently been in trouble, there had been a misunderstanding. It was a long story, during which Lina made tea, sliced a lemon and prettily put out some sweet biscuits. The voice droned on: ' ... and, well, there was I with my husband in prison and my daughter Kyra to bring up and educate. She had to go to her dancing lessons, there was a state scholarship of course, but how could I manage to make her frocks? To walk to the dancing class she had her bronze velvet dress with lace collar and cuffs, so charming, but ...' Whereupon Lina, careless of the woman's past plight, was quite carried away by the thought of the small daughter being taken to her state dancing class in a velvet dress and lace collar, in the sunny Muscovian spring-time. Lina, for all her twenty years at that time, felt a heart-yearning for Moscow, and spent many months brooding how she could manage a student-exchange or some sort of work permit to leave Bulgaria and go to the Soviet Union, to Leningrad even, or wonderful Moscow.

But her dreams fed on Serge's stories of London after that first night of his return, and on subsequent warm nights when they had taken a boat down the river all day under the blazing sun. More and more she wanted to hear about the 'sociology' of the West. She slept with Serge as if he was a bourgeois sea with the waves breaking over her. She told him she had found out a lot more recently about her father; he had been 'killed in the war' only so far as it was during the war that he died, and his calling had something to do with the court of King Boris, but he had not been in the army, he had been in the Bulgarian consular service; what he had been doing actually during the war in Venice, where they said he was buried, she did not know, since there never had been a Bulgarian consulate in Venice. Lina said she would like to find out, and meant to travel to Italy one day.

That would be a good thing, said Serge; she ought to travel. One could appreciate the Republic of Bulgaria better having been away for a while.

She already had a job as an art teacher in a secondary school. Many years after Serge's return, Lina managed to get a trip to Paris with an educational group tour. There, on the day before she was due to return, she left her hotel, left the group, went to the police station and defected. 'Name: Lina Pancev ... Sex: female ... Occupation: painter and teacher of art, advanced grades. Degree in Education 2nd Class,

69

University of Sofia, Bulgaria. Former residence Sofia, Bulgaria. The above-described individual states that she seeks refuge in the West for political and ideological reasons. We are informed that her group ... '

This had been a year before she met Robert Leaver in Paris. At first, she had caused a public stir; her name was in all the newspapers of Western Europe – 'Red Girl Painter Defects' and 'Balkan Woman Artist Makes Getaway': 'Lina Pancev a top Bulgarian artist was today reported to be in hiding under the protection of wellwishers after her defection Tuesday. Pancev, who also teaches art, left her group of Bulgar educationists, requesting asylum from the French government and pleading that she had been followed for over one year by the secret police and she "couldn't stand it any more". She made her bid for freedom at 11 a.m. yesterday and is being held in a secret location while her position is being clarified. Miss Pancev had declared herself fearful of reprisals by Balkan agents in Paris.'

She made friends with a girl ballet-dancer who had defected from Romania and a young man who had positively fled from Czechoslovakia; she was taken up and put down again by several hostesses of the art world; she was taken on a trip to London. She lamented the lack of her own former paintings which she despaired of getting out of Bulgaria: 'I have nothing to show. I can't get my work out.' She painted some men fishing in the Seine, but nobody bought her pictures.

Lina could never understand the illogic of the West. 'What have we defected for?' she used to say, along with some of the more obscure refugees from communist countries who used to gather together in certain cafés or sometimes in the Orthodox churches on a Sunday. In London, Lina thought that the char-women, going to work in Hampstead where she insisted on staying, were far too well dressed, not nearly shabby enough in comparison to the house-wives who employed them.

She was at first less followed by secret agents than she thought she was. Very hard, she tried to trace the address of 'Deborah', the girl-friend whom Serge had described with semi-ridicule. The glamour of that woman and all her circumstances which had so gripped Lina, grew as she looked from face to face; long hair, long skirts, no make-up, not very pretty, rich and with alimony, very careless, very untidy. There were plenty of Deborahs, no matter which was the real one. Lina was unable to make her own good hair untidy, but she went into long dresses. She had boyfriends and slept with them, always preaching at them, whether they cared or not, the evils of East–West détente – 'What have we defected for?' Sometimes she remembered Serge's white teeth biting into the peach on that summer evening far away.

5

At the invitation of the voice over the loudspeaker, Grace Gregory, the former Matron of Ambrose College, looked out of the plane window at the Alps below and, having found no apparent fault with them, returned her attention to her companion.

'Leo,' she said, 'I'm sure we're doing the right thing. I can't wait to get there. Poor Anthea, she's the injured party all along the line and I'm going to sort out those two debauchees there in Venice.'

'Well,' said young Leo. 'We'll have a good time, Grace, depend on that. I don't myself see that there's much to choose between the injured party and the other parties. It's all one and the same, isn't it?'

'Adultery,' mused Grace. 'Rather than fornication. Anyway, I'm a definite friend to Anthea and injury or no injury I'm going to add insult to it. Fancy her going to a private detectives' and giving them the story. She never had reason to go to a private detective when I was Matron at Ambrose. I used to keep Arnold temperate myself in the sick-bay when there were no boys sick. Otherwise he would have been a libertine. I remember so clearly the smell of hyacinths on the window-sill and the sparkling medicine-trolley. If Anthea didn't suspect it she should have, and been grateful. Well, all that's past, Leo, and I appreciate the reduction on the ticket and this opportunity to sort them out. Mary Tiller's a cook, Leo, a whole cook and nothing but a cook. I'm a Matron. That's the difference.'

'Oh, never mind them,' said Leo. 'It's Venice we're going to see.'

'Oh, the gondoliers!' Grace said.

'As a matter of fact,' said Leo, 'compared to the people in the rest of Italy the Venetians are very austere.'

Violet de Winter, chief agent of Global-Equip Security Services Ltd for Northern Italy and adjacent territories, had been feeling the pinch of modern immorality, as she put it. Over the past ten years her business, on the GESS side, had deteriorated by seventy-five per cent largely because unmarried lovers no longer chose Venice as the most desirable place to be together and, moreover, the lovers' husbands and wives no longer seemed to care if they did. 'The bottom has fallen out of the love-bird business,' she frequently told her old friend Curran, who, in his turn, had always found her useful in many ways.

The point about GESS was that they operated on a commercial basis, and Violet got ten per cent. She had a strict range of territory in which to operate. Everything about GESS was strict, especially her instructions within the territory. Violet's job was to:

1. locate the subjects (two or more, as may be);
2. find out as quickly as possible their financial status;
3. exercise persuasion on any rich or susceptible party;
4. if none of the subjects was really rich, drop the enquiry and report back to GESS.

For 'persuasion' read blackmail. In this way, GESS was able to pursue its policy of dealing only on a strictly commercial basis. For the most part, they regretfully told their clients that 'after prolonged investigations nothing of importance has emerged relating to your esteemed enquiry. Yours sincerely, [squiggle for signature] Global-Equip Security Services.'

Ca' Winter, the large palace on the Grand Canal where Violet still lived, was in a fair state of preservation. She owned part of it and gathered in the rents from several of the apartments. The other parts were owned by other people, and by the relatives of the dead Count de Winter whom Violet, an Englishwoman, had married in 1935 after meeting him in the Uffizi Gallery in Florence. Now, occupying a quite splendid flat in the palace, she considered herself to be one of the stones, if not the pillars, of Venice. At the same time she practised several small money-making activities, never letting any opportunity pass, such as the publicizing of an American art exhibition or a German film show. She worked hard at these jobs of public relations lest some evil should befall her;

a cosy study in her apartment was dedicated to files and card indexes. Maybe it was the memory of a hard-up youth that made her feel forever in need of picking up a small fee here and there. Certainly, the Countess de Winter had been left quite well-off by her husband, and although feeling the pinch compared to the old days, she still managed to keep her private motor-boat.

While Grace Gregory with her young friend Leo was high over the Alps on her way to foreign Venice, its waterways and its bridges, to sort things out, Violet's thoughts were on the discreet letter she had received from GESS which, being decoded, offered her the exciting prospect of a small job.

Curran was in no way objective about Violet de Winter. To him, who had known her as a young woman, she had improved over the years; to him, she was a late blooming person. What to him was the result of a long hard haul to improve herself from the sallow and sullen English girl he had known before the war, would be to a newcomer in her life a remnant of some braver and more glittering social personality. That she had been of service to Curran throughout the long years of their friendship made her features beautiful to him, now that she was sixty-four, beyond what they actually were. And she had attained, little by little, the power to infuriate him, whereas thirty years ago it had been the other way round.

The day after Violet got her missive from GESS came a telephone call from Curran.

'I heard you were in Venice,' she said.

'Naturally,' he said.

'Well, I just heard you were in Venice, that's all. Did you read about Carla's cocktail-party in Verona?'

'No, why should I?'

'It was in all the papers. Connie threw a vase at Ruffolo the sculptor and said he should have been a bricklayer.'

'Oh, yes, I heard about that. I—'

'Well, I was there.'

'Why are you boasting about it? I'd hush that up if I were you.'

'Well, Curran, it was something to see, I can tell you. I arranged the publicity. It was quite something. When are you coming over? Are you at the Lord Byron?'

'Yes. May I come now?'

'Not now. No, please don't come just now. Come at five this afternoon. I've got a job on; I'm busy. I'll send my boat over for you at five.'

'I can walk across the bridge at five.'

'But it's a filthy day. You—'

'See you at five,' he said.

At five in the afternoon it was still raining and a gale blew up making the dark grey sea send the ships anchored in the lagoon into a static gallop. The canals were at low tide, chopping up their smells.

Violet had her central heating well regulated; she had switched on the rosy lamps, and shut out the very watery view by drawing the silvery satin curtains an hour before the reasonable time. Curran thought how like Violet to do that. She always made her own environment. She seemed to rule

Nature, more and more as she got older. More and more he felt her to be his equal.

'Well, how is Robert?' she said when he had settled himself with a drink. The last time she had seen Curran had been a few months ago in his house in Paris, where Robert was still installed.

'Oh, he's left Paris. He's in Venice.'

'Then he's with you.'

'No, he's not with me. He's staying at the Sofia.'

'Oh, there! Why?'

'He found a room there,' Curran said, 'that's why.'

'Oh, he found a room there. Am I stupid,' said Violet, 'or am I right in thinking he left you and came to Venice on his own?'

'Well, you're right,' Curran said. 'He's interested in a girl he met in Paris. She came to Venice.'

'Is he interested in girls?' Violet said, rather coldly, and as if the whole idea of a young man of Curran's being interested in girls was too much to ask her intelligence to take.

Curran said quietly, 'Girl or rather a young woman. Over thirty. I should say ten years older than Robert. But still a girl, you know.'

'And what about her?' said Violet next.

'Her name is Lina Pancev,' said Curran. 'A refugee from Bulgaria.'

'Pancev, Pancev ...' Violet's eyes consulted the carpet and the window-curtains in apparent search for enlightenment. 'Pancev,' she said. 'That rings a bell. Pancev ...' She stared in front of her. 'The name rings a bell,' she said. And so

77

saying, she actually reached to the wall behind her shoulder and pressed the button-bell, so that her manservant came in with a dish of canapés and a 'Good evening' for Curran.

'We need some ice,' Violet said, and when he had gone she said, 'Pancev, Pancev . . .'

'Stop it, Violet,' Curran said.

'If I recall—'

'You do recall,' Curran said. 'And, what's more, this Lina Pancev is the same Pancev, same family; she's the infant daughter that was. She's looking for her father's grave and that's why she's in Venice. Robert has come to help her.'

'Oh God!' said Violet. 'Oh God!' Then she started to laugh, in little bursts, looking all the time at Curran as if to force him by her laughter to acknowledge the cause of it. But Curran did not respond. He looked at the drink he held in his hand, embarrassed and shocked. Violet said, 'Looking for her father's grave . . .' and laughed again. Curran smiled towards her. 'That's enough, Violet,' he said.

'She must be sentimental,' Violet said.

'I dare say,' said Curran. 'It's very probable.'

'You haven't met her?'

'No. But I want to get her a job. I expect you need a secretary-help, someone capable, to look after your files, let's say, for your fashion shows and so on, or to do a bit of shopping. Keep you company.'

'No, thank you,' Violet said as the manservant came in with the ice, and when he had left Violet said of him, 'He's leaving. Somebody's offered him better pay. It's always the same. You train them, then they get ideas.'

Curran said, 'If you want to keep servants there's only one way. Pay them double what anyone else will pay.'

'Well, I wouldn't do that,' Violet said. 'I'd think it immoral. Besides, I couldn't afford it.'

'Lina Pancev might help you out,' Curran said. 'She might make a good *au pair* girl.'

'No, thank you,' Violet said.

'I just thought you might do me a favour by taking her on,' Curran said.

'Oh, well, if it's a favour. But I don't think I'd like her. I don't like her already.'

'I can see that,' Curran said. 'And I haven't met her myself. But it would be doing her a good turn. You see she's pretty thick with Robert—'

'Oh, you want to get her away from Robert, or Robert away from her? How could I do that?' The doorbell rang downstairs and Violet went to the window where she parted the curtains to peer down at the landing-stage. The gale shook the panes and the water lapped greedily. She let the curtain fall, changing the climate back again.

'That was the wine arriving,' she said. 'It's Tuscan wine. It doesn't do it much good tossing around in this rough weather.'

'Robert,' said Curran, as if anxious not to lose the drawing-room climate again, 'is a not very nice young man. Rather nasty, in fact.'

'Well, drop him, Curran,' Violet said. She took away Curran's glass and refilled it with ice and whisky.

'I intend to set him on his way. I don't drop people, as you know. But I want to make it easy for him to go on his own way independent of me. I've rather monopolized him the last two years. A mistake. One does make mistakes, you know, and—' He stopped to allow Violet the opportunity of denying that he made many mistakes. She said nothing, so he went on, 'Robert. He's a nasty young man in his way, is Robert Leaver.'

'Leaver?' Violet said.

'That's his name,' Curran said.

Violet took cognizance of the lampshade, the drinks-tray and the carpet. 'Leaver . . . Leaver . . . ' she repeated.

'Don't tell me that rings a bell, too,' Curran said. 'It's quite an ordinary name. His father's at the Lord Byron just now—'

'Oh, yes, of course. I must say—' But Violet did not say anything more on this subject. Sometimes, in the past, she had confided in Curran the names of the people she tracked for GESS and he had even made helpful suggestions, although she had never gone so far as to explain the persuasion part of the job. But this time she said nothing about the Leaver who was cited in her message from GESS the day before. She merely laughed again, as she had at the mention of Victor Pancev's grave, and left Curran quite irritated.

But now, unexpectedly, she said, 'Bring Lina Pancev along to see me. I'll try to find some use for her.'

'I won't bring her; I'll send her,' Curran said. 'If you need some help with her pay, depend on me. I'll send her one of these days.'

'No, tomorrow. I want her tomorrow morning,' Violet said.

'You don't have to launch her in Venice society or anything,' Curran said cautiously, seeing that she had in the past taken on this service for him with some of his American friends' daughters, and one of his own nieces. 'Just give her a job.'

'Leave her to me,' Violet said.

6

It was to the Pensione Sofia that Grace Gregory and Leo made their way from the airport by water-bus. Leo had used the telephone at his travel agency in England liberally and cheerfully, after office hours, to find out the whereabouts of a Mr Leaver. Having made five calls to the most likely hotels and pensioni, Leo had been rewarded at the sixth: 'Leaver, yes, hold on. I will call Mr *Leàver*,' said the voice from the Pensione Sofia. At this, Leo hung up, secure in his belief that he had located Arnold. Later that day he arranged to take a week's holiday that was still due to him for that year. By studied overlapping of weekends the week was extended to eleven days; then he promptly had rooms booked for himself and Grace at the Pensione Sofia. He arrived home that night with this good news and two air tickets for Venice at reduced prices.

'Did they say Leaver, Mr and Mrs, or only Mr?' Grace said.

'I only asked for Mr Leaver. But I didn't talk to him of course. He's there all right. You'll soon find out all you want to know, Grace.'

'That Mary Tiller!'

Here they were, then, at the water-gate of the Pensione Sofia.

Leo was the son of a Cockney Jewish mother and an Italian father from Trieste who had settled in Britain during the war, become a naturalized Briton, and a prosperous dealer in foreign stamps. Leo was in his first job. He was stocky and strong with a head of Afro-frizzed hair and beard, both achieved by permanent wave. From among this dark woolly cloud his two bright eyes peered out and his sharp nose ventured forth. He was comfortable in his lodgings with Grace Gregory. She had always liked him when she was Matron, and for his part he found her company relaxing after his parents' efforts to push him up a social scale which largely existed in their minds only.

Grace, for the journey abroad, had dressed in an outfit which she felt was more suitable for Leo's travelling companion than her usual sensible clothes for Birmingham daily life; she wore blue jeans in a large men's size but still fairly tight, and a shaggy grey and white short fur coat. She wore a pair of large unnecessary glasses. At short notice she really had got ready for the trip as if she had looked forward to it all her life.

She came into the long reception hall at the Pensione Sofia with Leo a short way behind her; she went straight to the desk and looked round for service. Katerina and Eufemia sprang up together from their seats near by; a few visitors who were sitting there or passing looked startled for an instant, then stared. There was a feeling of alarm in the room. The porter dumped the bags on the floor, waiting till the new guests should be allotted a key. Katerina went behind the desk, and Eufemia, with a surprised question on her face, joined her.

'We have two rooms booked,' said Leo in his almost-native Adriatic Italian.

'In the name of Gregory,' Grace declared. 'I pay the bill, that is. My young friend here is Leo. Separate rooms. Naturally.'

'Are you the two English who made reservations?' enquired Katerina, staring at the booking-ledger in a stunned way.

Leo's eyes were wandering to the staircase. 'There's old Leaver,' he said, perceiving Robert Leaver slouchingly descend.

'That's young Leaver, not old Leaver,' Grace asserted in a voice which caused Robert to look straight over to the spot where Leo, his junior by six long years, stood bearded at the desk beside his amazingly befurred former Matron.

'Well, Robert,' said Grace across the room. 'Why aren't you in Paris? I hope nothing untoward has happened. When did *you* last see your father?'

'Grace,' said Leo. 'They need your passport at the desk.'

'I've come to see your father,' Grace went on. 'I believe he's staying here.'

Robert walked over slowly.

'Welcome to Venice, Mrs Gregory,' he said. He looked with enquiring hostility at Leo, who had handed in the passports and collected the room-keys from the bewildered proprietors.

'Don't you remember Leo?' said Grace.

'No, I don't.'

Leo said, 'I was in the first form at Ambrose when you were in the sixth, I'm afraid.'

'What are you afraid of?' Robert said.

'Nasty as ever,' Grace said, turning to include Katerina and Eufemia in the conversation. Their English was not up to all this. Katerina bade the porter take the couple to their rooms. Leo took up one of his bits of luggage, a huge blue-denim knapsack, and followed the porter.

'Your father?' Grace said over her shoulder to Robert. 'I've come here to find him. He's staying here, I understand with his cook.'

'They're not here,' Robert said, 'but if you're keen you'll find him at the Lord Byron.'

'See you later,' said Grace.

'Are you sure?' said Robert.

'Well,' said Grace. 'I suppose so, I'm afraid.'

Leo grinned back triumphantly at Robert.

'Hello, Anthea, is that you?' said Grace Gregory into the telephone. 'This is Grace.'

'Where are you?' said Anthea Leaver.

'I'm in Venice, of course. Leo and I arrived safely. A lovely little hotel called the Sofia. Beautiful rooms. It's run by the two sweetest ladies you could ever hope to meet.'

'Grace, this is costing money.'

'I won't charge you for this call, Anthea. Money's no object when I'm having a good time like this. I've been waiting for it all my life. Besides, the phone's cheaper at night. You should travel, Anthea. I can't tell you how sorry I am for you, sitting there in that dreary little room when we're all abroad and having a lovely time. Food and wine, you wouldn't believe.'

'What do you mean, "we're all abroad"? Who's "we"?'

'Well, Leo and I and everyone around. Would you believe it, Anthea, that the first person we bumped into was Robert.'

'My son, Robert? He's in Paris.'

'No, he isn't. He's in Venice staying at this hotel. And you wouldn't believe, I saw him again this morning with a girl looking at pictures in a church. The pictures are very much low-cut dresses and so on, but that's Italy, Anthea. You have to see it for yourself on the spot. I said—'

'Who was Robert with?'

'A girl. A girl about ten years older but still a young lady, you know. She looked a bit free, of course. He didn't introduce. I saw Arnold, Anthea, in St Mark's Square. He didn't see me as I ducked out of sight but Leo said he looked bad-tempered. Then Mary Tiller came along and they went into a café where the music was playing "My Heart Belongs to Daddy" outside. Tiller all dressed up. Of course I haven't had time to start finding out, but trust me to find out, Anthea. Not a word to that detective agency. Don't pay them anything whatever you do. You should see the Doges' Palace; you could put fifty drill-halls inside. I'll ring you again. There's Leo at the door waiting for me. I just wanted you to know that I'm thinking of your interests, Anthea.'

'He looked bad-tempered?' Anthea said.

'So Leo says. I didn't see him very close. Leo says Arnold didn't recognize him with his beard but ... '

When Grace had rung off Anthea got up and straightened the hang of the curtains; she then kicked a chair; she turned on the television news and watched it without taking it in. Then she dialled Robert's number in Paris. No reply. Usually there was someone in the place where Robert lived in Paris, care of Curran, but tonight the telephone fluted into great emptiness, rhythmically like an old barn-owl until it stopped and clicked over to the quicker hysteria of the engaged signal. Now she thought of getting back to the Sofia hotel in Venice which Grace had mentioned. It was altogether possible for her to do this through patient contact of Continental Enquiries, but no sooner had Anthea thought of it than it seemed too much; she knew it was her destiny, or she thought it was her destiny, which was the same thing, that she shouldn't know what her son was doing in Venice, or ever find out for herself. GESS was at work for her. Grace had arisen and gone abroad for her. Dizzy with this reasoning Anthea made herself some tea; she fumed at the thought of everyone having a good time, seeing the palace of the Doges and sleeping with each other in Italy while she was carrying on, keeping the home tidy, watching the electricity so that the bill wouldn't be too high, thinking of the cost of living here in the British Isles where people ought to be. But the moment of truth would surely come within the week. Mr B. of GESS would surely ... She took up her novel:

Matt looked enquiringly at Beryl with raised eyebrow. Since he and Joyce had been married he had not somehow felt so relaxed as he did tonight. Could it be the effect of the slow unwinding that preceded this hour, this moment? That process of inhaling, eyes closed, and knowing everything was going to be alright. Inhalation made you open up like a flower. He asked Beryl to marry him, to his own surprise. She lifted Mark from his cot. The child was coughing. Her arms were rounded, brown, beautiful.

'What about Joyce?'

'I'll talk to Joyce,' he told her. 'I think she'll understand.'

'And our children?'

'Well ... I don't know. Maybe I'll get a job ... '

Anthea's eyes drooped. And so to bed.

7

Violet had opened the curtains of her study to the clear bright morning.

'You look every inch an artist,' she said to Lina.

'It isn't what you look, for an artist, it's what you do,' said Lina.

'Oh, I know that! My goodness, I've known enough artists ... But there's something about you – I would have said right away, seeing you in the street, "That young woman is an artist." You know, when a woman is an artist, she is an artist in many other ways than in practising the actual art.'

Lina sat in a deep chair drinking her coffee and sizing Violet up. Violet was in another deep chair, opposite her, lolling. Lina had come about the job.

'As to your father's grave,' Violet said, 'I admire you for coming to Venice to find it. That's what I mean by an artist. I've lived in Venice many, many years. I know the Venetians.

I know Venice. I'm a bit of an artist myself, in many ways. I'm sure, in fact, I could help you to trace your father's grave. You need someone who knows the place, who knows the past. I'm sure we can help each other.'

'What sort of work?' Lina said. 'I can cook, Countess de Winter, but not fine cooking. I'm not French. I can do housework, but you have a spacious establishment to maintain in cleanliness.' Lina looked up at the high ceiling ready to defend her right not to climb up and clean it.

'Goodness!' said Violet. 'There's a woman who comes to clean. I'm losing my butler soon, but that's something else. To me *au pair* means equal and I would regard you as a friend if you want to come to help. In fact, in my sort of work, the need for domestic assistance takes second place. I was thinking of starting you off with an outside job. You see, I do a certain amount of research. For organizations. For a book . . . Tourist research. That sort of thing. You might call it sociology. Would you like to see the room at the top of the house that I thought you would like to have for a studio? Curran told me you would probably like to have a studio.'

Lina followed Violet out of the flat on to the landing of the wide public marble staircase. Violet led her to a small lift, but Lina stopped to look out of the window on the landing.

'You get a better view from upstairs,' Violet coaxed. But Lina's shiny black head was pressed to the window, watching some special thing, so that Violet looked over her shoulder to see what it was. A number of people were crossing the bridge on a side-canal outside the Ca' Winter. 'Anything special?' Violet said. Lina raised her hand. Then Violet saw a tall young man with curly brown hair lift his hand to wave back. He had been standing on the bridge, looking up.

'My friend, waiting for me.'

'Well, ask him in,' Violet said. 'Let him come in and wait. Is that Robert who's Curran's friend?'

'Robert Leaver,' said Lina. 'No, he won't come in. He likes to wait about. He's that sort of man. He likes to wait for me.'

'He's a very *young* man,' Violet said.

'He loves me,' said Lina.

'What does he do?'

'Only loves me. He's a student but not very much. He's ten years younger. I'm not in rivalry never with no one.'

'Oh, you've no need to be in rivalry, I'm sure. Well, let's look at your studio and not keep him waiting in the cold. You can have him to visit you as often as you like.' They were in the little lift now, going up. At the top Violet unlocked a large black door which opened into a vast bare attic.

'We can get furniture. Anything you want. I've heaps of stuff,' Violet said.

Lina looked round the room. Two windows lit one half of it. The other half was in a very attractive gloom as if waiting for an occupant to light it. 'What are my duties?' Lina said suspiciously.

'Oh, well,' Violet said, getting ready to leave the attic and lock up, 'let's go down and discuss your little duties.' But Lina lingered to look out of the windows which gave on to the back of the house.

'You won't see him from there.'

'I was admiring the panorama,' said Lina.

On the way down in the lift Violet said, 'As to your father's grave, you must give me all the details and I'll see what I can do to help. I can't promise results, of course.'

Lina said no word of thanks but followed Violet back into the study.

'I'm so happy,' Violet said, 'that you are an artist. There's something about a woman who is an artist ... Well, it's a matter of one's sixth sense, isn't it?'

'Which sense?' Lina said.

'I mean, as we say, sixth sense. We have five senses, all right. But some people have what you would call a sixth.'

'Ah, yes. I need some pay if I work.'

Violet looked sharply wounded, but only for a passing second. 'I could get a lot of rent for that studio up there,' she said.

'Oh, but I could never afford it,' Lina said, taking up her big shopping-bag, ready to go.

Stingily but with determination Violet bargained for thirty-five minutes more. Curran would undoubtedly pay Violet well for this favour, but that was no reason to throw money away on Lina. She would have been willing to go on for the rest of the morning, weighing the probability that Lina was anxious to get away to her waiting lover against her own haste to employ Lina as cheaply as possible as a spy for GESS; for Violet had lived all her life from one opportunity to another and now it seemed to her only right and providential that Lina should be induced to investigate the elder Leaver through her friendship with the younger. And since Violet usually had several subsidiary reasons supporting the main one for any particular course of action, she bore in mind

the possible usefulness of Lina in further, unforeseen, unspeci-
fied undertakings.

And while her reasons were only a web in formation, her
instinct was clear: the girl was in a weak position and far from
home. It should be easy to get rid of her if she proved useless.
Violet sighed. 'I can give you a little money, of course, if you
attach importance to money,' she said. 'I'm not a rich woman.
My old butler has been bribed away to Florida. I only want to
find some means to help you to find your father's grave. There
are people about in Venice, right at this moment, believe me,
who probably know the whole story of your poor father. They,
too, may be looking for his grave, would you believe it? There
are forces at work, Lina. I could give you a list of names that
would surprise you.'

On both sides of the garden of the Pensione Sofia were dotted
little circular flower-beds and shrubberies. Rose-bushes,
geraniums, Michaelmas daisies, and various types of chrysan-
themums were in bright bloom among dark leaves at grassy
intervals from each other. And on either side, too, one of the
larger flowery circles was surrounded by a gentle wire-hooped
protection about twelve inches high, as if the flowers within
those two particular circles were to be guarded more than the
others. This seemed possibly to be a relic of some former floral
arrangement. Lina and Robert walked up and down the
gravel path, not daring to tread on the grass, although there
was plenty of lawn-space between the flower-beds; it was
only that, being well-trimmed and cared-for, it had a forbidden look. Lina said, 'If this was my garden I would plant it

all wild and let everyone share it. It's nice to walk in a wild garden.'

He had been listening to her account of the interview with Violet. 'I told her I would think it over a few days. That made her angry. Why shouldn't I think it over? Anyway, besides, it is always good policy to say you want to consider.'

'Quite right.'

'Only she might take on someone else. I think I would like that job. She can help me to find my father's grave, and I am determined. She would give me a beautiful room in her palace but the pay is poor. I will keep her waiting some days.'

'Well, you don't need to work very hard for it, once you're in. Get your foot in the house, then set your own working-pace. Don't work for more than she pays you.'

'You know,' said Lina, 'the job doesn't sound very hard. She wants to know about people who come and go in Venice, so that she can compile data for her book on the sociology of Venetian tourism. It's real sociology she wants me to do, which is better than housework, as I thought. I was really expecting to be lady's-maid like part-time Cinderella; but you see I have to go out and study people, get to know them and all their business. Do you know, she suggested where I could start, and guess where?'

'Florian's café.'

'Well, that would be one of the places. But Violet said I should be advised to try the Lord Byron; and you know, Curran has been talking to her; your friend, Curran, they have discussed her book, and he has told Violet about your father, you know, and his woman.'

'She wants you to investigate my father?'

'That's right. There's nothing personal about it. It's only—'

'What a good idea,' Robert said. 'What a very good idea. Get the low-down on them, Lina. Get all the facts about them and put them in Mrs de Winter's book.'

'*Countess* de Winter; she said I could call her Violet. The book will only have case-histories but no names, you see. I don't know why you want to upset your father so much; after all, he is your father. I understand what you feel about the shamed woman, Robert, but your father is your flesh and your blood; if he was in his grave you would look for his grave like me.'

'I would dance on it,' Robert said.

'What's wrong with your father? Many men have mistresses, it isn't their fault. When you're older you will understand.'

'He can have twenty mistresses. I just don't like him.'

'But you like Curran instead.'

'No, I don't like Curran, either.'

'You love your mother?'

'Oh, God! I just never think of her. She doesn't count.'

'You must be an idealist,' said Lina. 'You are a man of vision. What do you do all day when you don't see me?'

'I'm working on a book. Maybe a novel.'

'Here is friends of yours, waving. Who are they?'

'Grace Gregory,' Robert said, 'with her Leo. Let's get out of here.' He took Lina's arm and turned her towards the garden exit.

Grace, however, caught up with them, her breath cheerfully

visible in the cold air as she said, 'Well there you are, Robert, with your lady-friend. Come along now, introduce us, here's Leo. We had a wonderful morning, didn't we, Leo? Let's all sit down on this bench. Sit down, sit down, what do you mean, it's cold? I'm Grace Gregory and this is Leo. What name did you say – Lina Pancake, ah, *Panchoff*. I always say foreign girls are good for a boy to start with, don't I, Leo? Oh, look there, over the hedge. It looks like a funeral.' Sure enough, coming up the side-canal was a funeral barge, gold and black, brilliant with flowers.

A Venetian funeral is intended not to be missed. Even the motor of the barge chugs with a mournful dignity. On the tip of the prow is a gilded ball with flame-like wings, signifying who knows what pagan or civic concept, but certainly symbolizing eternity. Next on either side of the wide black boat come two golden lions *couchant*. Then the windscreen, surmounted by vivid masses of flowers under which is posted the sombre, steady-eyed driver. Close behind the driver the men of the family stand, hatted, in dark suits. Then the coffin in the middle of the hearse, the lid covered with bright yellow and red flowers, and the wooden sides glittering with elaborate carvings. More enormous-headed flowers cover the cabin at the stern where the women mourn with black veils and white handkerchiefs. Another ball of eternal flames at the stern gives moral support to the general idea. And all this is reflected in the water beneath it: the stately merchandise and arrogance of Venetian death, as of old, when money was weighty and haste was vile.

Even Grace Gregory was impressed, exclaiming with

approval how, with a funeral like that, nobody could pity the dead one. 'I always hope that when my time comes nobody will come to the funeral and say "poor Grace". That's what I would object to.'

Lina remarked that she wished she could find her father's grave. 'Maybe he had a funeral like that.' Whereupon she and Grace, there in the garden, went into a series of avid questions, answers and explanations that lasted until Grace was apprised of the young woman's situation and plight, and long after the funeral barge had disappeared. Robert walked away. Young Leo hung round the two women, staring with much appreciation at Lina as she gave her animated account of her life to the present date.

8

An opalescent day, pink and grey. Lina was moving her light baggage and bundles, her square packages of canvases and painting-books, into the Ca' Winter. 'It's incredible,' she said. 'Robert promised to come and help me. I waited in all morning. I went down to the bar and I phoned his hotel Sofia. The lady answered; she said he wasn't in, his bed has not been slept in and so therefore he must have been out all night. I phoned Curran and he was out. Then I bought a coffee and a bun and went to the Hotel Lord Byron. Curran just came in. He didn't see Robert for two days. He said Robert wasn't with him. But I said I had this appointment this morning at ten. So we phoned the Sofia again. No sign of Robert. Now I did my moving myself as I can easy do. But I wonder where is Robert?'

'Maybe he's gone back to Paris?' Violet said, her eyes seeming to count the bundles and packages that had now been moved from the boat to the landing-stage and from there to the black and white squared floor of her elegant entrance-hall. 'Is this all your stuff?' Violet said.

'Yes, it's all mine.'

'I mean, is there any more to come?'

'Another boat-load, easy,' said Lina. 'Can you pay the fares? I don't have no spare cash.'

'Don't think me interfering,' Violet said, 'but that carton of kitchen stuff could have been left behind.' She was pointing to a large carton, bursting at its edges, which contained jars, tins and bottles of salt, vinegar, old pieces of soap that had been filched from public wash-rooms, toilet paper, a feather duster, three scorched pots, a black-looking frying-pan, a large bottle containing two inches of oil, a bottle with a half-used pink candle stuck into it, and other items of Lina's household goods. She said, 'The duster I need for my paintings; they should be cleaned only with the feathery duster which I need. I met Robert's father at the Lord Byron and his woman who is not so bad. She won a football lottery but that doesn't make her rich like Robert said. I can leave these things down here if you like as I have to go back for more, at least two journeys, and Robert is waiting for me I am sure. He is—'

'What was that you said,' said Violet, 'about Robert's father and his friend?'

'Curran introduced me. They had not seen Robert, neither. The father said he didn't know, didn't care. The courtesan was not so bad and, you know, Violet, she was help-ful to me, I must say. She said any friend of Robert's is a friend of hers. A real woman.'

'And the football pool? What did you say? She won a prize?'

'She is not so rich like Robert said she was. Only she won a football pool and that is rich for a cook, and it would be rich for me. But she isn't rich like a millionaire that stinks so much. Curran came back to my flat to help me with my belongings. Curran was kind to me. I know it's for the sake of Robert but it's nice just the same. He's got another boat coming with more of my goods right now.'

Violet stared at Lina as she rattled on. Lina was counting, checking, and shifting her bundles as she spoke, but Violet's ears had picked out one item only: Mary Tiller was not in the blackmail-rich category. This simple piece of information had come to her from the source she had employed to get it, and Violet, with her eyes on Lina's bundles, now wavered somewhat. 'Are you sure,' said Violet, 'that the lady-friend of Mr Leaver is not a very wealthy person? I understood she was. This is an example of the type of research I wanted you to do, Lina. You must be sure of your facts.'

'But I am always sure of all my facts. I will get facts from all the visitors in Venice. I was told it from Grace Gregory, who I met at the Sofia, an old woman who looked after the schoolboys when Robert was at school. She had a frizzy-hair boy with her, so dumb. Curran was laughing a lot when he told me of the mistress of Robert's father who is Mary Tiller. Curran likes her and he said she acts like she wants to spend all her money fast. I think like Curran that it's very humorous. I hope he brought my lard. I have a five-kilo jar of it that I got the butcher to prepare for me after the shop hours, cheap. Lard is important both for stomach and intestines. It also lubricates the lungs within the chest.'

'Lina,' said Violet, 'you know you should come on trial before bringing all your possessions along here. I'll give you a week's—'

'Here's Curran,' said Lina, peering through the glass doors. She opened them. A loaded water-taxi was approaching the landing-stage of the Ca' Winter, with Curran standing in the midst of a pile of fruit-boxes laden with objects and two arm-chairs which oozed stuffing at many points.

Violet went out, shivering in her jumper and tweed skirt. Curran smiled at her affectionately as if taking it for granted that she would share an indulgent benevolence towards Lina and her trappings.

'What d'you think of this lot?' he said as the boat bumped against the moorings.

'Look, Curran,' said Violet with a crack in her calm voice that made him look at her attentively. 'Lina is only on trial. I'm sure she doesn't want to come on a permanent basis until she finds out whether she likes it. And for my part, I—'

'Oh, I shall like it. I intend,' Lina said. She jumped into the boat to grab one of her boxes, setting it rocking and caus-ing the driver to shout.

'But it's all settled, Violet,' said Curran. 'I can't let Robert down at this point. I promised him I'd get a job for Lina, and you've offered her the job.'

'Don't worry, I'll be useful,' Lina said, puffing. She was carrying a large open crate, from which the top layer of con-tents, a hammer, an electric grinder, a mammoth-sized pot of paint and an Italian–English dictionary, gave a hint of the great weight of everything below. 'Where's my spirit-stove?' said Lina when she had dumped her box heavily on the lovely black and white square tiles of the hall. 'Oh, God, my tiles!' said Violet. 'My spirit-stove,' said Lina, 'must be somewhere. I need it for my travels if necessary. Most of my furniture I gathered here and there for my flat, but my spirit-stove is necessary for survival. I had it since I made my act of exile. Now, where is it?' Curran, on the landing paying the drivers of the two boats, stopped doing so; he helped Lina back into a water-taxi and followed her, to make sure the spirit-stove had not been left on the floor of either of the boats. One of the drivers shouted something, whereupon Curran told him to keep the change, helping Lina, with her long skirts lifted, to the landing-stage once more, still calling for her spirit-stove to the skies and to the waters. All of which was witnessed by various Venetians from the footpath and by some of Violet's elegant tenants from behind the discreet windows of their apartments in the Ca' Winter.

Violet now stepped forward and ordered the second driver to wait. She looked at Curran and said, firmly, 'All this stuff must go back. I can't have it here. I'll pay Lina a month's wages and let it go at that.'

'I've nowhere to go,' Lina said. 'I've rented my flat to an Ethiopian student. I've brought my belongings to your house. You gave me the attic studio and I have my civil rights. I fled my country and I got asylum. You have no rights on your side. The student has paid me three months' rent in advance, which is money that I needed, and it is my right to make my profit in a capitalist system.' She hauled the first of her bundles over to the lift and pressed the button for it to descend. She pushed in the bundle and heaved another package over to the lift. 'And I can help you with your researches, like you said you will help me with mine. Don't worry.'

'You promised,' said Curran, suddenly infuriated, 'to help her find her father's grave.' Violet stood still and dignified, as if the pink and pearl daylight were her natural backdrop. 'Her father's grave must be somewhere in Venice,' Curran said somewhat emphatically. Violet looked at Curran and they smiled at each other. 'My spirit-stove,' Lina said, pouncing upon it where it lay behind a box. 'Now I go up to the top and I come down again for the rest. If you hand over the key, I know my way,' said Lina.

Later that day Violet sent off a telex to GESS which, decoded, read: 'Friends at Hotel Ld Byron. She won two hundred thousand in a lottery two years ago otherwise penniless. Please instruct but must warn operational costs this end increased twenty-five per cent.'

9

The attic studio in Ca' Winter was such that Lina had dreamed of sometimes, before she left Bulgaria, when Serge had been recounting his stories of life in the western countries. She had since actually seen grand and spacious attics like this, with adequate windows, northern lights, in Paris and in London, and had seen their pictures in films. These wonderful studios were always in the hands of expensive-living people, sometimes of an arty turn, sometimes not. Poor artists, she had found all her life, were no longer able to afford these attics of character atmosphere as Lina described it to Violet as she looked round her new studio the day after she had moved in. The vast space available to Lina's tattered belongings swallowed them up so that they looked nothing like so desperate as they had on arrival. Violet had put in a divan bed, completely overcome by Lina's determination to exist in these surroundings. 'This is a good attic apartment,'

Lina told her. 'You must have money to throw away, that you haven't rented it before, but I commend you for handing it over to me. The bed is too narrow, it is a single person's bed only. I hope I can help you in your jobs and your sociology in return for all this atmosphere.'

'I already told you,' Violet said as she looked round the room, 'that I could get money for this attic.'

'But you don't care for money,' Lina said, agreeably.

'I have to care. But this big room has memories. Personal ones. I like to keep it available for myself. You can only have it temporarily.'

'First I make some memories for myself,' Lina said.

Lina had already, the previous night, shown herself eager to be of service in Violet's establishment; the only thing she would not hear of was that she should not have her attic. Last night, Lina had descended from her attic to the kitchen where she not only mended an electric iron but cooked a good meal made up of rice and pieces of fish, which she had served and eaten with Violet, who had thereupon made up her mind to make the best use she could of Lina.

Now, in the morning, she stood surveying what Lina had done to the attic. 'I wouldn't bring your boy-friend up here to sleep,' she advised.

'Why? Are you jealous?'

'My dear, what would I want with that boy?'

'I mean, jealous for me. There must be some reason you wanted me so much to come here. You want me?'

'No, thanks,' Violet said. 'That's not my way of things.'

'Just as well,' said Lina, 'because my boy-friend wants me.

I have to call him. Where did he go? He should have helped me to move in here.'

'Maybe he's left Venice.'

'Why do you say that?'

'Well, if you say he didn't sleep in the Pensione the night before last, well, perhaps he's just gone off. Young men do go off.'

'But he left his clothes. Only he didn't sleep there. He must have spent the night somewhere else. Could be, with Curran.'

'Could be, with Curran,' Violet said. 'Would you mind doing some shopping for me? Are you a good shopper?'

'What shopping?'

'Well, the grocer, and mainly, this morning, the butcher. People coming to dinner.'

'I know good butchery when I see it,' Lina said. 'So you give me the orders and the money, and I can go across to the Pensione Sofia to find Robert, too. I have told him he must be a man of vision and I can make him one.'

Grace Gregory found Arnold, that morning, sitting gloomy and solitary in the lobby of the Hotel Lord Byron. 'At last!' she said, sitting down heavily in the chair beside him.

'What are you doing out here?' said Arnold, who, in his younger days, had spent some time as a teacher in Kenya.

'Quite a fancy place, this,' said Grace, looking round the hotel lobby. 'It must be expensive.'

'I'm on a holiday,' said Arnold. 'Did Anthea, or did Anthea not, send you to spy on me?'

'Anthea knows where you are. It's hardly for me to spy on you. Anthea just wants to know your future plans. Do you intend to have a permanent liaison with the cook?'

'You're jealous, Grace.'

'Ah, that's what they all say. At least I protected you. Anthea knows nothing about us. She knows all about Mary Tiller. I saw Anthea, beginning of the week. Her nerves are at—'

'Breaking-point, I know, I know,' he said. 'So are mine. And I come here for a holiday ... What do I find? First thing, Robert hanging round the reception desk, looking like a male tart and poking his nose into our business. Second comes Robert's rich friend Curran, insulting me in my own bed-room. Number three, along you come, all the way out here to Venice, where I'm on my holiday, and you bring up Birmingham. I want to forget Birmingham. I'm under orders.'

'Whose orders?' Grace said.

'My doctor's orders.'

'Oh, I thought you meant the cook's.'

'And you must please not call Mrs Tiller the cook. Cookery is chemistry. Mrs Tiller is a very intelligent companion.'

'Well, Arnold,' said Grace, 'I can't say you look as if you're enjoying her company. You've lost your twinkle. You used to have one.'

'A what?' said Arnold.

'A twinkle in your eye. It's a lovely day and you're in Venice. Nice and brisk. You should see the art-work in the galleries!'

'I've been to the galleries.'

'When you had Anthea to go home to at nights you used to make the most of your days. You look like a long draught of pump water. I wonder what Anthea married you for. Here's Leo.'

'Good morning, sir,' said Leo.

'Who are you?' said Arnold.

'Leopold Leopoldi,' said Leo.

'A former pupil of Ambrose,' said Grace.

'I recall the name but I wouldn't have recognized you,' said Arnold looking with some distaste at Leo's two eyes and nose which were all that presented themselves for recognition amidst the frizzed foliage of black hair surrounding them.

Leo sat down. 'Robert seems to have cleared off,' he said.

'Back to Paris?' said Grace.

'Good,' said Arnold. 'Wherever he's gone, that's one of you the less.'

'I don't feel we're welcome,' Leo said, settling himself further in his chair. He had a bunch of picture postcards in his hands, and now started to write to his friends.

'Well, Grace, you might as well have a drink,' Arnold said, having softened a little at the news that Robert had left Venice. He even included Leo in the invitation. Leo accepted without looking up from his card-writing.

'Tomorrow, Sunday, I'm going to ring Anthea again. You get it cheaper, Sunday. Have you any message to send?' Grace asked him when they had been served their drinks.

'Why do you ring Anthea?'

'To keep her advised as to her state of wedlock,' Grace said.

Leo looked up for a moment with bright eyes, then went back to his card-writing.

'This is persecution,' Arnold said, looking round the room.

'Mary Tiller's in the hairdresser having her roots done,' said Grace. 'So I shouldn't think she'll be back for some time if that's who you're looking for.'

'If I want to tell my wife Anthea anything,' Arnold said, 'I can ring her myself. In fact, I might do. Now, suppose we agree that you spend the rest of your holiday with this young man and enjoy yourselves, and leave me alone to enjoy my holiday, too?'

'Venice is a small place,' said Grace.

'Well, Mary and I will be moving on somewhere else. That's all I can say to you.'

Leo made one of his rare comments; he had looked up from his postcards to sip his beer. 'Oh, good!' he said. But it was immediately apparent that he was referring to Lina who had come into the hotel laden with plastic shopping-bags.

'I come to you,' said Lina, 'with my grocery and flesh, because I had to do my shopping for the Countess. You know, I had to walk to the other end of the island as I am acquainted with the cheap shops there. I know an old butcher, he makes me up my lard since I was in Venice. The Countess Violet likes cheap, it will make her pleased. But I took the *vaporetto* back as quick as possible to see you.' She sat down beside Leo and dumped her shopping on the table and the floor. 'And I must tell you that I went also to the Pensione Sofia to find Robert. Two nights now, he hasn't been to his room, and his belongings are there still. He's missing since Thursday and the ladies at the Pensione say that they haven't heard. Curran was there, too, looking for him. Curran says it's typical of Robert just to walk away and leave everything, and not to worry. But I say we tell the police.'

'I agree with Curran,' said Arnold. 'My son is irresponsible.'

'Thoroughly irresponsible,' said Leo placing a comforting hand on Lina's.

'While I'm here,' said Lina, 'I ought to snoop. It's part of my job.'

Arnold looked round the room. 'Mary should be back soon,' he said. 'I've been waiting an hour.'

'I don't need to snoop on you,' Lina assured him. 'I know all about you already.'

'No,' said Violet on the telephone, 'he hasn't been here. Lina was expecting him to call or phone. I expect she's gone off with him. She should have been back with the shopping.'

Curran said, 'Yes, I saw her at the Sofia. But she hasn't found him. He's not there. He hasn't been back for two nights.'

'Are you anxious?'

'No, only curious.'

'See you tonight at dinner. Eight o'clock.'

'Eight o'clock,' said Curran.

10

When the weekend passed without any sign of Robert, nothing at all, no message, nothing, Curran went around the
vicinity of the Pensione Sofia making a few enquiries. 'It is
not,' he explained to Violet on the telephone, 'that I am
responsible for Robert. I am not condemned to take care of
him. Only the girls, I mean Katerina and Eufemia, say it's
their duty to inform the police, it's the law and so on.'

'Has he got his passport with him?'

'Oh, yes. He always carries his passport when abroad. He
could have gone anywhere. It's all rather typical ... Draw
attention to himself ... A real damn nuisance ... Lina and
who? Lina and Leo. Who's Leo? Oh, well, I haven't time to
think about their affairs. Let them sleep with each other all
day, all night; I only want to know if she's had any message.
Typical of the young, they don't care what happens to their
friends, they just fall into bed with someone else ... Yes,

Violet. I know we were young once ourselves but we had some sense of behaviour, and we had feelings. I'm not going to be condemned to spend my time looking for Robert. No, he isn't in my flat in Paris; my man there hasn't seen or heard from him. There are a few bars here in Venice where they might know something, near the Sofia. He used to hang around ...'

The prospect of going around the bars alone asking for Robert did not appeal to him after the first try. 'I'm looking for a young student; he was here last week. Name, Robert Leaver. Tall and thin, twenty-four, brown curly hair and a moustache, nice-looking.' The bartenders and the groups of multi-national students looked at him, some replying with cynical indifference, some with plain resentment and with amusement, too. It was not a good idea. Curran went to the Hotel Lord Byron and claimed Mary Tiller from under Arnold's eyes just as the couple were about to set off for their morning coffee at Florian's in St Mark's Square, like so many others.

'I'll come, too, if you insist on taking Mary. I'll make enquiries everywhere. I'm the father,' Arnold said. 'I don't know why I should do it, but I will.'

'That would be the worst thing you could do,' Curran said. 'There would be a lot of gossip and nothing accomplished. If he's made friends in Venice they certainly won't tell his father where he's gone. Then the police are always hanging around these bars, you know, in plain clothes, dressed like students. They'll imagine he's on the run.'

'Well, he is on the run.'

'No doubt,' said Curran. 'Then let him run and don't antagonize him. He's free to do what he likes.'

'He has no money,' Arnold said.

'Oh, yes, he has. I gave him some,' said Mary.

'Look, Arnold,' said Curran, 'you take a trip to one of the small islands. They're very picturesque. Torcello, for instance. Mary and I can just go around on Robert's usual beat, explaining that we're tourists, we've come to Venice and we're looking for a young friend.'

'He might have gone back to Paris,' Arnold said.

'I know that. He might be in Turkey, anywhere.'

'Arnold, don't fuss,' said Mary.

'If you're going to spoil our holiday like this, Mary,' Arnold said, 'I shall return to England.'

'Oh, no,' said Mary. 'I'll be back this afternoon. There's nothing, really, to be anxious about, but it's only that Curran wants to know, and the people at that Pensione want to know, naturally.'

Arnold finally let himself be put on a boat to Murano, with instructions to buy some small glass objects as presents to take home.

'It would have been too bad, too unfair to Robert, to let him start making enquiries,' Curran said. 'A lot of these students are English-speaking and so are the Venetians. Robert would be furious when he came back to know that his father—'

'If he does come back,' said Mary. 'In my opinion he's left for good.'

'Did you give him much money?'

'No, I've only got my travellers' cheques with me. I gave him seventy pounds. I'm sorry I did, now.'

'He won't go far on that,' Curran said. He himself had given Robert a great deal more, only last week.

'He didn't ask for it, either,' Mary said. 'I just thought he might like it, to take his girl out to dinner, you know.'

'Don't worry,' Curran said. 'Robert isn't short of money. He could always go where he liked, all the time.'

They made a rough radius of the Pensione Sofia, trekking through the narrow, crowded streets, the alleys, round a few squares and across bridges, enquiring for Robert wherever they found a group of young people. Many of these groups were of mixed nationalities. Curran and Mary together managed to make known their quest. Generally, the Venetians in the streets and in the bars were fairly obliging. They hesitated, took time, made suggestions, or wished the older couple good luck in finding their friend.

Curran, after two hours, four drinks and two espresso coffees at various bars, began to show his irritation at the lack of results; he was used to a fairly quick response to his demands; ideally, one pressed a bell and something began to happen; he began to feel appalled at the total nullity of the quest so far, and the probability that the two hours could be extended to eternity. It occurred to him to wonder if, should he catch sight of Robert himself standing on a bridge or leaning on a counter in a bar, he would not prefer to walk on, ignoring him. To Mary, he said, 'We've been at it for two hours.'

'Over two hours,' said Mary. 'If I'd known, I would have

put on different shoes. My heels are a bit high for walking.'

'I hate to be defeated,' Curran said. 'We should at least go to the University and fish around there.'

'You know,' said Mary, 'you and I, Curran, are very much alike. I was just thinking we should go to the University, and I also hate to be defeated.'

Curran knew that her mind was not really set to the purpose when, on the way to the University, she said, vaguely, 'We could, of course, try the hospitals. You know, he could have been run over, or something . . . '

'What by? A gondola?' said Curran.

'Or he could have been taken ill.'

'He's in the best of health,' said Curran, 'wherever he is. You can be sure of that.'

They took the water-bus to the nearest stop for the University and walked around for some time without seeing many students. Those whom they approached knew nothing of Robert Leaver.

'My feet are tired,' Mary said. 'Why didn't you bring Lina? He must have been seen with her. Someone might remember her by sight.'

'I thought of Lina,' said Curran, 'but to be quite honest I don't feel I should draw her into this at the moment. There's nothing to be absolutely alarmed about, you know.'

'Do you really want to find Robert?' Mary said.

'No, not particularly,' Curran said. 'You're a clever woman, aren't you?'

'But you just want to make quite sure he's gone.'

'Something like that,' Curran said. 'It would be a damn

nuisance, too, if the police started making enquiries. It isn't a police affair.'

At a students' eating-house, they found an American girl who seemed to remember Robert; at least, he was called Robert and fitted the description. She had met him in the library just off the Santa Maria Formosa, but that had been sort of last week. They had left the library together, walked around the church. 'I think he was studying the church of Santa Maria Formosa.'

'That's right,' Curran said.

'Well, I think he was sort of thinking of writing a novel.'

'A novel!' said Curran.

'Yes, I think so. Kind of, with that part of the city as a background.'

'It's quite probable,' said Mary. 'They all write novels.'

'Oh, yes,' said Curran, 'quite typical of Robert,' and he looked at the American girl, a lumpy girl with an open shiny face, and asked her, 'What next?'

'Oh, nothing. I had a date and I just said, you know, good luck with your book. I didn't see him around since.'

'Thank you,' said Curran. 'Well, I expect we've missed our friend; he must have moved on.'

'I guess so,' said the girl.

Mary and Curran decided to go back to the Pensione Sofia. 'Maybe we could question some of the guests,' Mary said.

'The two women have already done so. Nobody remembers him very much, and many of the guests who were there last week left at the week-end; new ones came.'

On the way back they stopped for lunch at Curran's

favourite restaurant near the Pensione Sofia. There, without prompting, the waiter said to Curran, 'Where's your young friend?' It occurred to Curran that in any other circumstances this would have been indiscreet. But now he responded eagerly, 'We're looking for him. You haven't seen him by chance? Has he been in here lately? The last few days?'

The waiter gave thought to these questions, screwing up his eyes. 'He's left his hotel,' Curran said, 'and we don't know where he is.'

'I saw him ...' said the waiter. 'Oh, yes, it was Thursday, our day of rest. We close on Thursdays. I was out – where did I see him? He was ... yes, outside the church of the Santa Maria Formosa, talking to some people. I greeted him as I was passing. I remember he turned and saw me and said "Buon giorno", that's all. It was about midday on Thursday last.'

'The people he was with, who were they?'

'I don't know who they were, but I think Italians, Venet-ians, not tourists. There was a middle-aged man and a young woman.'

'The man rather short and the girl a bit taller, with long blonde hair?' Curran said.

'Yes, that's right. I think so.'

'Well,' said Curran, to Mary, 'that brings us up to Thursday, anyway. Let's order our lunch.'

When the waiter had gone Mary said, 'Who are the people Robert was talking to?'

'I don't know,' said Curran. 'But I saw them several times following Lina, then they started following Lina and Robert together. I thought it was Lina they were after.'

'You know,' said Mary, much revived by a few sips of the wine Curran had poured out for her, 'you are making my holiday, Curran.'

But Curran wasn't thinking of her holiday. 'He was seen talking to these people on Thursday at noon,' he said. 'And he didn't go back to the hotel on Thursday night. I hope he's not going to make a damn nuisance of himself. I hope he isn't up to something.'

As soon as they entered the hall of the Pensione Sofia, Katerina said, 'Curran, there's a letter addressed to you. Someone left it on the desk.'

The envelope was typed. Curran looked at it before he opened it, and said, 'Who left it?'

Katerina said, 'I don't know. Eufemia and I weren't here.' Curran realized as she spoke that Katerina was agitated and was doing her best to conceal it; after all, he had known Katerina for a long time. He opened the letter. It was typed:

Curran, you're making a fool of yourself going round Venice in that company. The blonde is a husband-poisoner. You have been going around enquiring for me. Your sweet old friends Katerina and Eufemia are advised not to inform the police of my disappearance. Side-effects might ensue such as exhumations, etc., etc. From there would follow the implications that touch on your complicity. Collect my things from my room in the Pensione Sofia. You're to pack them yourself and keep them in some safe place. I have been kidnapped. You are to pay the ransom. My custodians will be in touch with you by telephone. Tell everyone only that you have had a letter from me to say I have gone for a trip to an undisclosed destination, that I don't want to be followed, that I don't want to be looked for. Prepare the money. It has to be a lot, I warn you. Several million dollars. They know everything. As I do. When I am released, I can promise you that it is over between us. It will be goodbye, goodbye, goodbye,

ROBERT

The signature was Robert's or very like it. But Curran spent no time studying this or any other detail. He folded the letter and put it in his inner pocket. Mary had sat down and was attempting to make conversation with Katerina, who stood by, fidgeting with the edge of her pullover and watching Curran eagerly.

'Isn't it peculiar,' said Mary in a voice which was rather shrill in an effort to make herself understood to someone not English, 'how the beauty, the great beauty, of Venice simply changes when one has some worry on one's mind. Take this morning, for instance, when we were looking high and low for this young man, Robert, it wasn't so enchanting as it was the other mornings when I went for walks in Venice. The beauty simply—'

'It's from Robert,' Curran announced. 'He's all right. He got a friend to drop the letter in; very obliging of him. He asks me to pay the bill and collect his belongings. So that's what I'll do, Katerina.'

'Yes,' she said, 'that's the best. I can get that done for you right away. Eufemia said she hoped we wouldn't have to tell the police.'

'But where is he?' said Mary, looking at Katerina as if finding it somewhat curious that Katerina herself had not asked this question.

'It's infantile,' Curran said, sitting down beside her. 'I'm afraid Robert's behaving in a quite infantile way. But it's quite simple really. He says . . . he says . . . ' Curran pulled the letter out of his pocket and scanned it casually. 'He says . . . "Tell everyone that I have gone for a trip to an undisclosed destination, that I don't want to be followed, that I don't want to be looked for." Those are his very words. Pompous, infantile. Anyway, at least we can forget him, now. He asks me to take his belongings. I'll get Violet to look after them. Well, Mary, we might have saved our shoe-leather and our breath.'

'Could I see the letter?' Mary said, holding out her hand.

'Oh, later, later,' Curran said, putting it back in his pocket. 'I'll have the key to his room, Katerina. I'd prefer to do the packing myself, since he asks me to do so. Where's Eufemia? One of you had better come with me to make everything correct. I don't suppose he has anything valuable, but I want to make a list, and I'll give you a receipt.'

'Eufemia's in bed with a headache. She's taken a bad turn,' Katerina said, in Italian.

'Speak English,' said Curran. 'Mrs Tiller is present.'

'I understand a good bit of Italian,' Mary piped. 'More than you think.'

'The Signora understands Italian,' Katerina said.

'That's what I thought,' said Curran. 'But we don't want to be rude, do we?'

One of the clients was at the desk waiting to pay for some postcards. Katerina went over to serve him. Then she said, pointing rather angrily to the rows of pigeon-holes, 'The key to number 28 isn't here. The maid must have taken it.'

'I'll wait for you,' said Curran. 'We'll go up together.'

'But I can't leave the desk,' Katerina said. She buzzed on the intercom, evidently to Eufemia's room, and spoke in rapid Venetian, from which it emerged that Eufemia was by no means able to rise from her bed at that moment. Katerina said something final and harsh-sounding, and banged down the receiver.

'I can wait,' Curran said. 'What does the maid want with the key?'

'She has to tidy the room.' Katerina was distraught, with a number of people now crowding round the desk.

Curran sat down beside Mary. 'You'd better get back to the Lord Byron,' Curran said. 'Tell Arnold that there's nothing more to worry about.'

'He isn't worried. He won't be a bit surprised that Robert's walked off like this. Arnold thought that's what he'd probably done. I'd like to come and help you pack.'

'There won't be much. He travels light,' Curran said. 'I have to pay the bill, and so on. Please do go ahead. I'll join you later.'

After many protests he at last persuaded Mary to leave. Just as she was going out of the front door, in came Grace Gregory followed by her bright and hairy Leo. This caused

Mary to change her mind and turn back, all eager as she was to be the first to impart the news from Robert. It was just on four o'clock when afternoon life was starting up again. People were coming downstairs; they were coming in the front door and going out of it; they were crowding in the hall, going out to the footpath and coming in from it. Curran sat mutely with the letter burning in his pocket, while Katerina frantically coped alone with the guests who wanted postage stamps, and with the telephone-board that kept buzzing with incoming and outgoing calls.

Grace pushed through the crowd towards where Curran sat at a low round table which was covered with some sensational Italian glossy magazines of an old and ragged date. He lifted one of them as if he hadn't recognized Grace, although he had seen her on one of her sallies to the Lord Byron. But he glanced up as she came to his table followed by Mary and Leo. Mary was still in the process of recounting their morning's hunt. 'And then,' said Mary, as she crowded in on Curran with Grace and Leo, 'when we got back here there was this letter for Curran from Robert. My dear, the fatigue ...'

Curran stood up, while Mary introduced him. The women settled themselves in the chairs beside him; there was no chair for Leo, but he stood in a vacant space blocking, as it seemed to Curran, the only route of escape. 'And you see,' Mary rattled on, 'Arnold was right after all. Robert simply went off, leaving all his stuff for us to mop up. It's really very inconsiderate of him, even though, between ourselves, it's understandable if you remember your own young days. I feel like a drink. Is the bar open? Oh, yes, of course it's open, I forgot; this is Italy. I wouldn't say no to a gin and tonic.'

Curran was looking at her abstractedly as if he hadn't heard. But he pulled himself together when Leo, who was ready to go and fetch the drinks, put his hairy head close to Curran's face, saying 'Place your order, *please*.'

'Whisky on the rocks,' said Curran, getting out his money which Leo waved aside. Grace put in for a nice sherry.

'Many a nice sherry,' said Grace, when Leo had gone to the bar, 'I had at Leo's expense one time at Ambrose College where I was Matron, when he brought back from half-term a large medicine bottle labelled "To be taken twice a day before meals". But it didn't fool me. One sniff and I could tell it was the very best sherry, medium-dry. So I confiscated that item and enjoyed every drop of it; and while we're talking about confiscations I brought off another coup this morning. You'd never guess what I found upstairs in Robert's room. I just thought—'

'Here, in Robert's room?' Curran said.

'Yes, well, as he's gone AWOL I thought I'd just pop in and enquire, but there was nobody at the desk, it was half-past eight this morning so I helped myself to the key. As a former Matron I feel it's my right to know. Well, there wasn't much. Only a few clothes and his notebooks. No drink, drugs or money. But I found some notes for a novel he's writing and believe me, it's a revelation into his mind. I've only had time to read the first two pages because I like to take it easy, you know, but—'

'You had no right to touch anything,' Curran said. 'I'm

afraid you'll have to hand over the notes, Mrs Gregory. I have a letter from Robert authorizing me to pack his belongings because he's gone away on a trip to a destination that he does not wish to be disclosed. It's really quite a serious thing to go into someone's room without their permission and take their property. It's breaking and entering. It's—'

'No, it isn't breaking and entering,' Mary said. 'I know that for a fact, Curran. It's only entering without due consent. The law—'

'Mary, perhaps you know the laws of England better than I do,' Curran said. 'No doubt you have reason.'

'Oh, plenty of reason,' Mary said. 'I've been burgled twice. Why don't you show Grace your letter of authority from Robert? I'm dying to see that letter. Here come our drinks.'

Leo came, followed by the lanky boy who tended the bar, carrying the drinks. Curran rose and went over to the desk where Katerina was for a moment free from any of her guests. 'I'll have to wait till these people are gone,' he said, 'but it seems that Robert Leaver is going to give us trouble; we must talk.'

'Eufemia had a phone call an hour ago,' Katerina said. 'I must tell you—'

'Wait till later,' said Curran. 'I want to pack Robert's things. But now I've just heard that Mrs Gregory – that's the old one in the fur coat and blue jeans with spectacles – went up to his room this morning and took some of Robert's papers. They might be important. Would you mind stepping over to our table and asking her politely to return them?'

'Oh, no, I won't do that,' Katerina said. 'I tell you it's best not to show fear. There is a book that Robert is writing. Eufemia got the message, all of it on the phone. Robert is writing all about us because he knows all about the past, all of it. I don't want to be involved.'

'But you are involved,' Curran said.

'It's a threat,' Katerina said.

'Of course it is,' said Curran. 'Why did you give the key of his room to the maid?'

'I have the key to his room,' Katerina said. 'I have it in my pocket. No one else can enter.'

'Well, his room was rifled at eight-thirty this morning. You were too late,' Curran said.

'But how could I know so early? We didn't get the call till after lunch.'

Curran returned to the table where Mary was describing in elaborate detail a Renaissance Italian recipe for a sweet sauce comprising cane sugar, vinegar, pepper and spices. 'Around the year fifteen hundred,' she was saying, 'they used a lot of spices which have practically been forgotten and herbs which, you know, were probably the same as our forbidden drugs, not to mention the poisoning that went on. My dear, if you read your—'

'Mrs Gregory,' said Curran. 'The proprietor of this establishment wants those notes back, and any other thing that you took from Robert's room. She is entitled to inform the police of an illegal entrance to her clients' rooms.'

'I should think Robert's father is the one who should have the say,' Mary said. 'But I don't see any harm if it's only notes for a novel he was writing.'

'It's a very unnatural piece of work,' Grace said. 'I must say, so far as I've read, he names names. But that's just like him, to make up stories about the people who've been good to him. I tell you, Mr Curran, what I'll do. I'll hand it over to you when I've read it. I don't think it would be fair to hand it over to Mr Leaver Senior, really I don't. How low can one sink? I have to ring Anthea tonight cost what it may. I couldn't get through last night at the cheap rate. She doesn't know Robert's gone away. But good riddance to him, that's what I think. Well, Mrs Tiller, I've been glad to meet you again for a talk face to face. Come along, Leo.'

'Tell Anthea,' said Mary, 'that her husband is in good hands.'

Curran swallowed down his whisky.

Mary was gazing upward. Then she said to Katerina, 'Allow me to pass a compliment on your beautiful chandelier.'

11

Monday night. Violet handed back Robert's letter to Curran after she had read it. They were together in her study at the Ca' Winter.

'It's the word "exhumation" . . . ' she said.

'That affair of Pancev had nothing really to do with me,' Curran said. 'I was only trying to help.'

'Me too,' said Violet. 'I wish I didn't even know about it, I hardly remembered much about it, as a matter of fact, until Lina Pancev turned up. It hadn't crossed my mind for years and years . . . I've had other things to think about.'

'Did you notice that phrase "the implications that touch on your complicity"? Ghastly pompous phrase, and he means it. I would have thought it was a hoax, but really . . . '

'Well, you must know your Robert,' Violet said.

'Whoever has told him about Pancev is deliberately misinforming him in order to blackmail me,' Curran said.

'Oh, undoubtedly it's the Butcher who's got hold of him,' Violet said. 'I suppose the Butcher needs more money, now that the cost of living … Katerina and Eufemia have been paying the Butcher all these years, but of course they don't have a fortune like you.'

'I had nothing to do with Pancev's death. I dined with Pancev at the Villa Sofia the night before he died. I had the shock of my life when I heard. I liked Victor Pancev.'

'Oh, I know that he was killed by those Bulgarians. But I'm terrified of what Robert can say.' She was sitting very straight in her chair. She looked rather wooden. 'I got a letter, too,' she said. 'It's clear that Robert has got a true bit of the story, or perhaps two bits, and is prepared to elaborate the rest.' She opened her little purse, took out a square-folded piece of paper, and handed it to Curran. She got up and arranged the curtains of her small study, pink and mauve English chintz, quite a different background from that of her drawing-room. She looked out on the lamplight and darkness without noticing whether it was raining or not, whether the wind was blowing, cold or warm, she was indifferent to what was outside as if she were young again, unbothered by the weather and concerned only with the atmospherics of her own senses. She straightened the cosy hangings. 'I can't believe this is happening,' Violet said.

Curran's hand gestured for silence while he stared at the letter.

… know you, although you do not know me, except for one time we met in Curran's flat in Paris. It has been

brought to my notice that both you and Curran were
co-responsible in the year 1945 AD for (A) the
vivisection of Victor Pancev, and his subsequent burial
in two parts of the garden of the then Villa Sofia now
Pensione idem. (B) You were the lover of Victor Pancev.
(C) Curran was an agent for the Germans. He turned on
Pancev, who had been involved in a German plot to
poison King Boris, and arranged for Pancev to be killed,
to silence him. (D) Curran is involved with yourself in a
drug racket. Exhumations and revelations might ensue if
you, Countess de Winter, do not persuade Curran
quickly, repeat quickly, to prepare a substantial sum of
money. I am in the hands of armed kidnappers who will
stop at nothing. Phone call to follow.

ROBERT LEAVER

P.S. You and your late husband, Count Riccardo de
Winter, were also spies for the Germans 1942–1945.

'Vivisection,' said Violet, 'is not true. He was already dead.'
'Drug racket is not true,' said Curran.
'You were Victor's friend,' said Violet.
'And you were his lover,' he said.
'There's the question of the body,' said Violet. 'The rest is
immaterial.'

Curran said, 'The owners of the Pensione are answerable.
We should go straight to the police with these letters. Let
Katerina and Eufemia take care of themselves. We should go
straight to the police. Vivisection, indeed. Drug racket, indeed.'

'They would dig up the garden of the Pensione Sofia. If

Robert starts this smear, how are we to escape from it? God, I'm frightened. The stories would be all over the place. After all, we were both *there*.'

'Robert isn't working alone, you know,' Curran said.

'Oh, obviously, it's the Butcher. I got the letter in a plastic bag that Lina brought back with the shopping. She didn't know it was there.'

'Might she be involved in this?' said Curran.

'No, the Butcher is just a butcher to her. She doesn't know where Robert is. She knows nothing about her father, how those two women fought over his body. She knows nothing about life, nothing about art, nothing about anything . . .'

'Keep calm, Violet,' said Curran, not being very calm himself.

'A pair of savages,' Violet said. 'And after all they've paid the Butcher all these years—'

'The police,' said Curran.

'And maybe,' said Violet, 'there are people who remember that Riccardo worked for the Germans when they were here. Who didn't? But the police would never believe we weren't involved in the murder, and drugs and any other crimes we're accused of. They would dig up the two halves of Pancev's body and we'd be interrogated, the house would be searched, you would be hounded in every country. This isn't England, you know, and even there—'

'It's the Byzantine Empire here,' said Curran. 'I wish I could see Robert and have a talk with him.'

'You must have a lot of faith in him, to say that,' Violet said. 'Or else, faith in yourself. Personally, I think he's evil.'

'So do I,' Curran said, 'and infantile. Which amounts to the same thing when you add a little power. Only a little power.'

'The police searching the house, making enquiries ... I couldn't live through it, Curran.'

'You shouldn't be mixed up with that unsavoury outfit, GESS,' Curran said. 'That's something you don't want known.'

'There's plenty you don't want known, Curran,' said Violet.

'That's exactly what Robert is counting on,' said Curran.

'Robert and the Butcher,' Violet said. 'Do you think it possible he's written these missives under duress?'

'I don't think for a moment he's been kidnapped. I think they've got hold of Robert because they know he's my protégé. They want money, that's all.'

'Then give them money.'

'He talks about millions, plural. A million isn't what it used to be but from Robert's point of view it's a career. Even one million, never mind the plural. If I paid a cent where would he stop? You must be mad. Let Katerina and Eufemia pay if they want to hush up their ridiculous secret.'

'They haven't got millions. I could never see what Victor Pancev saw in them. A couple of housemaids. But they were fiercely in love with him. I wish I'd never been mixed up with Pancev. What's a body?'

'But you helped them,' said Curran. 'You found the Butcher for them.'

'No, I didn't.'

'If your memory is honest,' said Curran, 'I think that you did. I always assumed,' said Curran, 'that you were furious, after he was dead, to find he had been sleeping with them as well as with you. He had energy, did Victor Pancev.'

'Do you want to quarrel with me?' Violet said. 'Because, if so—' The telephone rang just then. Violet looked at the clock. 'Nine-thirty,' she said as she went to answer the phone. 'I should have been at the committee meeting for the Liberation of the Environment.'

The call was not from the committee meeting; it was from Grace Gregory.

'Excuse me, Countess Winter,' said Grace, 'but I've mislaid Leo. Is he there? This is Grace Gregory speaking, onetime Matron of Ambrose, friend of—'

'Leo is with Lina in her studio. There is no telephone there,' Violet said.

'I can well understand how upset you feel,' said Grace. 'That young woman is insatiable. I've hardly been able to have a word with Leo since he met your Lina, and—'

'She is not my Lina,' said Violet. 'She is Curran's protégé. He wished her on to me. He's here in—'

'Insatiable, that's what she is.'

'It's in the family,' Violet said.

'Well that's interesting. I've been reading some notes about the father that Robert Leaver, vile young man, left behind in his room. I confiscated them. I have to talk to Curran about them.'

'I'll pass you Curran.'

'Well, I was debating whether I could come to your place—'

'Curran,' said Violet. 'Mrs Gregory on the line. Please take over.'

*

'Lovely place you've got,' said Grace.

'Of course, there isn't a word of truth in it,' said Violet. She was referring to the close-typed, rumpled, pages of notes in her hand. She stared at them, with Curran looking over her shoulder, while Grace stared round the drawing-room.

Résumé   *Quest for Victor Pancev*
                        Past History

1936–1938 AD

Paris and Venice

Curran, a young wealthy American expatriate.

Violet, English wife of Riccardo de Winter, a luxury-living Italian fascist.

Victor Pancev, a Balkan diplomat close to the then King Boris of Bulgaria.

The above are part of a luxury fascist-bourgeois set who meet in Paris, London and other luxury capitals, leading a life of luxury and irresponsibility.

1943 AD   The Germans have occupied Bulgaria. King Boris dies of poison. V. Pancev is suspected of complicity with the Germans in the murder. V. Pancev, fearing the revenge of the royalists, transfers to Venice, which is occupied by the Germans, leaving behind his wife who early in 1944 gives birth to his daughter, Lina.

In Venice, V. Pancev lodges at the luxury Villa Sofia, home of an elderly count. Two young women, Katerina and Eufemia, look after the villa. They are possibly the Count's illegitimate daughters because when he dies the following year (1944) the two 'maids' inherit the luxury Villa Sofia.

V. Pancev loses no time in seducing first one and then the other of the sisters. Unbeknown to each other, both Katerina and Eufemia fall madly in love with Victor Pancev, who is attractive.

He has also lost no time in taking up his friendship with Violet and Riccardo de Winter who live in the luxury Ca' Winter and who also are German agents. V. Pancev also sleeps with Violet who is madly in love with him.

1945 AD   The Allies take Venice and the Germans go away. Very soon after the British and New Zealand troops occupy Venice, Curran arrives as an American liaison officer. He has spent the latter part of the war in the American Army but he has been working for the Germans and Italian fascists as an underground agent as his old friends the de Winters and Pancev well know. He takes up abode at the Villa Sofia.

The night after Curran's arrival in Venice he shoots and kills V. Pancev in the garden of the Villa Sofia where the latter has been lying low, because he is wanted by the Allied Forces intelligence for interrogation. Curran, who has been working for the Germans, has a motive for murdering his old friend of his luxurious youth. The motive is to silence Pancev. Curran has confided his plan to Violet and

134

Riccardo de Winter who also have reason to silence
Pancev about their activities in the German spy
network during the war.

Curran looked, frowning, towards Grace. 'It wasn't at all
like that.'

'It wasn't like that at all,' said Violet.

'That's how a lot of these young people talk,' Grace said.
'It's a fashion. They have this claptrap that if you polish your
shoes you're a fascist bourgeois. That's why I decided to travel
looking lefty. You never know when you need someone young
to help you if you're stranded with your suitcase.'

But Violet and Curran were reading on:

To avoid an open enquiry Curran proposes to bury Pancev
in the garden of the Villa Sofia.

In the middle of the night he informs Katerina and
Eufemia that a man's body is in the garden, and that he
was probably murdered by Bulgarian royalists or by
Riccardo de Winter in jealousy of his wife's lover. Curran
advises them that in either case they would be better to
avoid a scandal and to co-operate with him and the de
Winters in burying the body in the garden.

But while he is telling the sisters all this they have an
unforeseen reaction. They rush to the body and start fight-
ing over it. Katerina claims it and Eufemia claims it, each
declaring that she alone was Victor Pancev's lover. Curran
as a bluff threatens to call the police, which frightens the
women who have been guilty of harbouring Pancev and

have also been helping Violet and Riccardo with their German underground activities. But the girls (as they then were) continue to argue as to whose side of the garden he is to be buried on. Curran telephones to Violet and Riccardo who come over in their gondola to try to calm the women down, but to no avail.

Violet then has the idea of sending for her friend a fascist butcher. Riccardo goes off in the gondola to fetch him. He arrives with his apprentice armed with meat hatchets and they slice the body in two. Before dawn Pancev is buried on both sides of the garden, half and half.

When asked later what happened to their pre-war luxury friend Victor Pancev, Curran and the de Winters always answered that he was murdered either by avenging Bulgarian royalists or Italian partisans.

In 1953 Riccardo de Winter dies leaving his luxury palazzo to his wife Violet.

Curran is never suspected of his role as a German agent. After the Allied armies are demobilized he takes up residence again in Paris where he continues his pursuit of works of art and youths. His aunts in America die like flies and leave him one fortune after another.

Just recently the Butcher died. The one-time apprentice, now his partner, took over the business.

Present Day. Venice

'It's a complete fabrication with our names in it,' Violet said.
    'I'll make him change the names,' Grace said, 'when he

comes back from his travels. You wait. There's such a thing as libel.'

'There is indeed. Just what I was thinking,' Violet said.

'Poor Eufemia and Katerina. Those dear, dear ladies, to link their name in connection with anything so bloody macabre. Only a Leaver could think of cutting up a body, though I've heard that the Turks used to kill their enemies by the scimitar with one swipe through the sternum. It makes you sick to think of, doesn't it? But read on. You haven't heard the half.'

'The half?' said Violet, all nerves, thinking of the body, her eyes on the notes.

'Half the story,' said Grace.

Violet and Curran were already reading on, but Curran paused to say 'This document reminds me of the first time I went into St Mark's when I was twenty years of age. I wondered if I was drunk or was the floor cockeyed. It's hallucinating.'

'The pavements in St Mark's were made to be wavy, according to my guidebook,' said Grace. 'Then they were restored with the rest of the church but some of the original crookedness remains.'

'I was probably drunk, too,' said Curran absently, as he continued to read Robert's version of the original crookedness.

'St Mark's,' Grace was saying, 'is quite something, isn't it? Of course, it's RC and it stands out a mile.'

'There you are – he says again that Mary Tiller's a poisoner. I wonder—' Violet said.

'Again?' said Grace. 'Did he say it before?'

'Only in passing,' Curran said, not intending Grace to know the contents of the letter he had received from Robert. 'But, of course, he would say anything.' Curran continued his silent reading.

But Violet looked up sharply. 'My God, I forgot! Lina's arranged for her to come and cook a dinner for ten tomorrow night.' She had come to the bit under '*Present Day. Venice*' where Robert had written,

> Among the new associates of Violet and Curran is the mistress of the father of Robert Leaver, whose name is Mary Tiller, a middle-aged fascist-bourgeois woman poisoner whose three husbands . . .

'You mustn't take it seriously,' said Grace. 'After all, it's only a novel isn't it? It won't ever get written. They never get further than five pages. You should see some of the beginnings of novels I've confiscated in my time; words wouldn't describe them. They usually write up to chapter two, but I've also seen this type of fiction drafted out in notes before. It generally all boils down to blood and sex. But this is the first time I've confiscated a literary effort that puts in real people's names. It's sick, very sick. Have you come to the bit about me?'

'Just coming to it,' said Violet, as she read:

> Grace Gregory, a former nightclub stripper of (*c.*) 1930 AD, at the height of the bourgeois-fascist London ethos, later contracts a marriage with one Gregory who has a licence

to run a public house in Norfolk. Grace, now 'reformed', is active in church affairs and hobnobs with the vicar and the local landed gentry during the fascist-bourgeois class-war of 1939–45 AD, being admitted into the company of that class solely because their servants have been transported to the battle-fields and the factories, so people like the imperialist lackey-collaborator Grace are the only remaining raw material for exploitation. Naturally, she is the vicar's concubine. Grace also continues to run the profitable public house in the absence of Gregory, who is killed in action 1944 AD . . .

'Why does he put AD after the dates?' said Violet. 'It sounds creepy, like a history book or a memorial stone.'

'That's the effect he wants to achieve,' said Curran. 'It makes us old and wicked.'

'Have you come to the bit about me and Leo, Venice, Present Day?'

Curran said, 'I don't want to read any more of this propaganda.' He went over to the drinks trolley with his shoulders bending a little, not his usual posture. He looked as if he were carrying the weight of all his own faults, but willingly, seeing that those attributed to him in Robert's scandal-sheets were so exaggerated, so unbelievable. And yet so dangerous in the utterance, for there remained the undoubted pieces of truth buried in the mixture, like the bones of Pancev under the garden-beds of the Pensione Sofia. He looked at Grace with a suddenly sweet and protective smile and asked her what she would like to drink.

Violet looked up from her reading. She was on the last page. 'Yes, do take a drink,' she said, '. . . quite forgot to ask you before.' Then she went on reading.

'The trouble is,' Grace said when she had got her glass of sherry, and Curran had settled in a chair with his whisky, 'that in fact I used to do a dance-turn, but I wouldn't call it strip. I was in the entertainment business as a girl like many another of talent. So far so good. But my poor husband, Mr N. Gregory, was a fireman and rose to be a chief-inspector in the fire brigade and sit behind a desk, so it's all wrong about him running a pub, not that it's any disgrace. However, true enough, during the war I helped in the bar at the Coach and Crown. As for village concubine, well, there were plenty of those but Grace Gregory wasn't one of them. Poor Mr N. Gregory died of a stroke. He was very much my senior, and we never spent time apart as he wasn't away in the war. Now, I got the job as Matron at Ambrose as a widow. But the story that Robert goes on to tell, as of me and the boys, well that's a bit of cheek.'

'Oh, quite,' Curran said. 'No one would believe it.'

'I'm not so sure of that,' Grace said. 'Give people a story and they believe it, especially if there are one or two authentic facts and dates. Do you know what? – About eight years ago, that is when Robert Leaver was still a boy at school, there were a few months when my rooms were often gone through behind my back. I never missed anything. But someone rummaged especially through my old memory-files, like letters and policies, sort of thing. I think it must have been young Leaver who got in there. Then, even when he'd left, some of the other resident teachers complained. There was nothing missing, only rummage. I almost suspected at the time, because only the cleaners had the use of the keys and the extra keys were in the housemaster's office, and the key to there came from the head's office. It's an easy guess after the event but you know, Robert Leaver was the headmaster's son and it didn't seem possible, I didn't want to think . . . '

Violet had come to the end. 'It's frightening,' she said. 'If he writes a novel, even without our names—'

'He wouldn't have left those notes behind if he was going to write a novel,' Curran said. 'He left them behind deliberately for us to see. He hasn't got it in him to write a novel.'

'All the same,' said Grace, 'it's slander and I would see a lawyer if I wasn't a friend of Anthea. Poor Anthea, she's been waiting for my phone call. I didn't get round to it last night; I didn't know what to say.'

'Better say nothing,' Curran said. 'Leave the parents out of it. Robert is a fool. For my part, it's not that I don't suffer fools gladly, but that I don't suffer them at all.'

'Sooner or later,' Grace said, 'the Mum and Dad will want to know where he is.'

'Well, we don't know where he is,' said Violet firmly. 'He's gone away and he can stop away.'

'Poor young Lina, to leave her like that . . .' Grace said. 'What will she do without him? She's the type of female that needs a man.'

'She seems to be doing very well without him,' Violet said.

A long loud female scream broke out somewhere in the palazzo from an upper region. The sound of a door being flung open so that it banged with an echo against the stone wall of the landing. This was followed by another anguished scream which seemed to curl down the well of the stairs to settle with a horrible 'Ah-ah-ah' outside the door of Violet's flat.

'Whatever is that?' said Grace.

Another scream, a bang, a man's voice protesting, trying to placate. Violet precipitated herself out to the landing, in time to see the little lift descending and, through its glass windows, Lina with her head thrown back dramatically and, her hands clutching her head, giving out frightful animalistic noises. Two of Violet's tenants from the floors above – one, a small elderly lady who had always been considered up to this moment to be totally deaf, and the other, a white-haired professor of music-ology – looked over the banisters of the staircase proclaiming their amazement and enquiring the cause of the rumpus as the howling lift descended before their eyes.

The lift passed the upper floor of Violet's apartment and reached the ground floor of the building. Violet, followed by Curran, had run down the flight of stairs to meet the descending lift, while Grace, outside Violet's landing, joined the banister audience.

Lina flew out of the lift, still yelling wildly, barefoot, dressed in a huge yellow flannel nightdress and throwing her arms around in a way which was quite alarming to watch. Violet caught hold of her, and Curran, too, tried to hold her, both joining the exclaiming chorus of the people above in the tall, echoing palazzo. 'What's the matter? . . . Lina, what-ever's the matter? . . . You'll catch your death . . . Stop . . . Wait! . . .'

But Lina had struggled free in a flash and had opened the front door. She ran out on to the landing-stage. She turned with her back to the water for just a moment in order to cry out 'Leo is the son of a Jew – I have slept with a Jew – God, oh God! – I must cleanse myself! I die for shame!' And with a further shriek the girl half-turned and dropped into the canal.

Leo had appeared by this time, having evidently run down all the stairs after her. He was naked except for his great head of hair and his beard, and he grinned continuously while he jumped into the canal after Lina, fetched her a blow on the head so that she stopped howling; he fished her out with the aid of Curran's outstretched hand. Curran then brushed the water off his trousers. An old-fashioned gondola passed by, empty. The gondolier shouted joyfully to Leo, 'Bravo, nudo!' and barge-poled ahead up the canal, rather precariously, for his head was turned back to Violet's well-lit landing-stage and the engaging spectacle thereon.

While Lina was being carted indoors, choking and dripping, Leo, usually so silent, went to the edge of the canal, cupped his hands and called over the water to the receding gondolier, 'Una nevrotica!'

At which the gondolier waved, shouted back something encouraging, and turned away about his business.

12

'Is that you, Anthea? This is Grace.'

Anthea had that morning received a letter headed GESS of Coventry in red letters, with a signature that looked like a large scrawled number 56 or, maybe, 85, but nothing else.

Dear Mrs Leaver,

Re your esteemed enquiry, after conducting in-depth investigations, we have to report that nothing of importance has emerged with regard to same.

Assuring you of our best attention at all times.

Yours faithfully,
[squiggle]
Global-Equip Security Services

Enclosed with the letter was a folded brochure. She glanced inside contemptuously in the desperate pre-knowledge that there was nothing else, no private message, absolutely nothing for her, after all her deliberations and summoning of courage to consult the people. The brochure was the same that Anthea had read at the offices of GESS while waiting for her interview with Mr B.

Missing persons
Backgrounds checked
Polygraph (Lie Detector) Examinations
Complete Crime ...

She threw it on the table beside the letter. It was eleven on the Tuesday morning of the third week of Arnold's absence. 'In-depth investigations,' Anthea muttered, and went to put on the kettle for her mid-morning instant coffee and, this being Tuesday, to clean out the goldfish bowl.

She had just finished the goldfish and was about to make the coffee when the telephone rang.

'I waited all Sunday night, I waited last night, and you didn't call. What's going on?'

'Well, Anthea, everything here ... it's unbelievable.'

'I can quite believe *that*.'

'Anything wrong, Anthea?'

'Oh, no, nothing wrong. Only my husband's in Venice with another woman and everybody's enjoying themselves stepping ashore from the gondolas like the Queen of Sheba except me.'

'Anthea, I want to talk to you about Arnold—'

'We're talking at the expensive rate. I can't undertake to

reimburse you for calls made outside the cheap rate. I waited Sunday and I waited—'

'Let me tell you for your own good, Anthea, that there's nothing wrong with Arnold and there's nothing really the matter with Mary Tiller. What you have to realize is that our generation has to stick together, no matter our differences, Anthea.'

'What generation?' Anthea said. 'You could give me fifteen years.'

'I mean, Anthea, people who you could give twenty-five years to.'

'Oh, that generation . . . I don't know what you're talking about. The young are perfectly sweet. Take my son, for example. Robert and I have a perfect relationship.'

'Anthea, have you heard from Robert?'

'No, I haven't. The last I heard he was in Venice with you.'

'Well, he isn't in Venice with us, Anthea, any more. He's walked out on everyone including his kind friend Curran, Anthea. He's left his belongings in his hotel room and gone off into the blue, Anthea. Curran paid up his hotel bill, Anthea.'

'Why do you "Anthea" me like that?' said Anthea. 'What's going on? My son must have gone somewhere. Where—'

'He said he didn't want anyone to know, Anthea, and I just wondered if you'd heard from him. He doesn't want anyone to look for him. I suppose that means you. Well, what I want to say mainly is that Mary Tiller is a very nice—'

'It all sounds very far-fetched,' said Anthea.

'It may seem far-fetched to you, Anthea, but here everything is stark realism. This is Italy.'

'Yes, and the phone bill . . . I've got the kettle on the gas. I'd better—'

'Would you believe it,' Grace said, 'that at the Pensione Sofia they haven't one single clue as to how to make tea? I said, "You take the teapot to the kettle, not the kettle to the teapot." But of course they use those bags. Then they were surprised at me having my lay-down after lunch under the table. I said, "It's good for your back. I've always done it all my life and as a girl I was a dancer on tour." I said, "This isn't the first time I've travelled," I said, "and it won't be the last. I always have my forty winks underneath the table." So they let it go at that. Young Leo went off with Robert's girl, but of course she's into her thirties so what can you expect? She's a foreigner, too. I mean, even for here, where everyone's a foreigner she's a foreigner. Some kind of Russian refugee but she may well be a spy because, to tell you the truth, she's not one of those persons you read about who go into exile for their convictions. Mary Tiller likes her and Curran – you know who Curran is, don't you? The rich—'

'I'll turn off the kettle,' said Anthea. 'Don't hang up.'

When she got back, Grace said, 'I'd better run along, Anthea, because the bill will be running up. I just wanted you to know that Arnold's in good hands when you think of all the worse things that could happen in this life. Leo and Lina, that's the Bolshy girl, fell out last night. Mary Tiller gave me a recipe for a special mutton stew, if you can find the mutton

147

these days, and it's a big If. What a pity you spent all that money going to those private detectives, Anthea—'

'I spent nothing,' Anthea shouted. 'And I want to know exactly what you're driving at. Where's Robert?'

'I'm doing all this in your own best interests, Anthea,' Grace said. 'How should I know where Robert is? You can't hold on to him for ever, can you? He's gone away and he doesn't want to say where's he gone. And if he's turned out to be a bad lot, well, it's nothing new. I always said—'

'Where is Robert? Where is that man Curran?' Anthea yelled.

'Calm down, Anthea, Robert's gone off as I say. Nobody knows where he is and for my part—'

The line broke down at this point and refused to be connected in spite of Anthea's frantic beating on the receiver-rest. Forty minutes later she got through to the Pensione Sofia and asked to speak to Grace Gregory. She was told that Mrs Gregory had gone out. On demanding to know if Mr Robert Leaver was there, the woman at the other end, in bad English, told her abruptly that they had never heard of such a person, and hung up.

The brochure from GESS lay on a little table beside the telephone, its fold half-open, positively looking at Anthea. She opened it fully, once more.

> Missing persons
> Backgrounds checked
> Polygraph (Lie Detector) . . .
> Complete Crime Laboratory . . .

Missing persons. Anthea made up her mind. Mr B. had seemed to understand her when she had gone to his office. Then it seemed from his letter that he did not understand her. She felt sure that, with the disappearance of Robert, she could make herself understood. She made her morning coffee and drank it reflectively.

That afternoon she stepped out with the courage of her wild convictions and the dissatisfaction that has no name.

'This Mrs Gregory that I'm telling you about was a very good friend but the trip to Italy has gone to her head. She rings me up in a patronizing voice, and tells me that my son has disappeared to nowhere and my husband's lover is a very nice woman. She takes up the attitude that I'm a back number who doesn't know life. As if we don't have goings-on here in England, sex changes, drugs and orgies. Don't we?'

Mr B. of GESS nodded.

'But Grace,' said Anthea, 'makes out that right is wrong, and I don't know what. She went to Venice to fetch my husband home. Now she tells me that Mary Tiller's a nice sort of woman and that Arnold's in good hands and that my son, Robert, has gone off all on his own, nobody knows where. She makes out all this is normal.'

Mr B. glanced at his watch. He had agreed to see her, very reluctantly, without an appointment.

'My dear Mrs Leaver,' he said. 'We have fully investigated the case as we said in our letter.'

'Well, I want to find my son Robert. Please start a new investigation.'

'We have no territorial rights in that area,' said Mr B.

'Well,' said Anthea, 'the gentleman with whom Robert resided in Paris might help you there. He has the entrée to many foreign places, in fact the geography of the world, you might say.'

'Then surely,' said Mr B. with his smile that was a no-smile, 'he is capable of locating your son himself. You have no need of us.'

That Anthea was anxious not to be dismissed was evidently apparent to him as it was that he was probably dealing, a second time, with a proposition that was beneath the dignity and profit-potential of GESS.

Anthea was thinking, now, of nothing beyond a need for hypnotic Mr B. to take her under his wing once more, as he had seemed to do on their first meeting. It didn't help that in other circumstances her common sense would have restrained her, for these were not other circumstances. She knew instinctively what to say in order that Mr B. should continue to give her his attention and look after her, so to speak. 'My son's friend, Mr Curran, is an elderly playboy. I doubt very much that he would trouble to look round the world for my Robert.'

Mr B. did respond. '*Curran?*' he said. 'Curran, the American art-collector?'

'That's right,' said Anthea, 'A multi-millionaire. He took a real interest in Robert. My husband would never have understood that fact if l e had known.'

'You didn't,' said Mr B., opening a side-drawer in his desk, 'give me any details of your son, Robert.' He brought out a number of little folded blank cards and placed the homely little regatta on his desk. Then he pressed a button and spoke into a flat instrument beside his blotter, 'Please bring me archived cards Leaver.'

When the old cards had been brought in, and arranged in a fashion that made Anthea feel almost happy, he took one of the new cards and wrote on it 'Robert Leaver'.

'Robert Leaver . . . ' he said as he wrote. 'Now, Mrs Leaver, why did you not want to tell me about your son in the first place?' He lifted one of the old cards and, looking at it, shook his smiling head. He observed, 'You were singularly reluctant to talk about your son.'

'Mr B., I'm a mother.'

'Oh, yes. He has something to hide. You have something to hide on his behalf. You see, Mrs Leaver, you should tell me everything. If you had told me everything it is probable your son would not have gone away without leaving an address.'

'I only thought of my husband and the rich widow. I only wanted to know—'

'Rich widow,' Mr B. said, 'Mrs Tiller is not, in any appreciable terms. Certainly, she is a woman of substance but I hardly think money is a great factor in her relationship with your husband, apart, of course, from the possibility that she has provided the wherewithal, shall we say, for the little escapade at Venice. Your husband just wanted a little change, you know; we all need a change. If I may say so you are a very wise woman, very sage, might I say, in turning your attention to your son, Robert. The fact that he goes off on a journey is not in the least unusual, nor is it uncommon for a young man to go away, leaving his belongings in the hotel and omitting to pay the bill. Especially if he knows perfectly well – and here we come to the crux of the matter – that the belongings will be collected and his bill paid by some good friend. And that good friend, if I may hazard a guess, is the American millionaire, Curran. Now, I see, Mrs Leaver, that your real concern is not that your son has gone away, but it is the relationship he has with the man, Curran. Am I right?'

'I don't know,' Anthea said. 'Perhaps we should leave it for a while. I don't want to interfere with my son's friendships. He wouldn't like that. I only wanted to find out where he is, and your brochure has got "Missing persons" on it.'

'How long has your boy been friends with Mr Curran?'

'About two years. He has a room in the gentleman's flat in Paris.'

'And you haven't wondered why?'

'Oh, no,' said Anthea. 'I haven't wondered at all. There's no need to go into all that.' She had lost her courage and looked really frightened. 'I'll have to sleep on it,' she said. 'Excuse me for the trouble. But as you say it's very, very normal for a young man to go off by himself. He might return quite soon, all the better for it. You see, he can't go far because he has no money.'

'Are you sure?' said Mr B.

'I don't know. The young people don't need money very much these days, do they?'

'Don't they?' said Mr B. 'Have you ever wondered where Robert got things, like for example his Cartier gold watch?'

'How do you know about the watch?'

'This establishment is GESS,' said Mr B. with a smile overtaking his built-in one. 'So you see I made a *guess*. Now, Mrs Leaver, if you don't want us to proceed to find your son, what did you come here for?'

'I don't know,' said Anthea. 'Perhaps I made a mistake. I'll think it over.'

'If you're afraid that you might get Robert into difficulties, or may I say awkwardness, please be assured. We are discreet, professional. I think I can help you in this case. I really think I can. So think it over well.'

'My husband and Robert don't get on well together,' she said.

'That's not unusual.'

'Oh, I know it's a very normal situation. You make it sound all so normal I really don't know why I troubled you.' Anthea stood up, looking from Mr B.'s face to the door, then back again, and again to the door, as if uncertain whether she longed to stay and talk it over or whether she longed to go.

'Sleep on it, Mrs Leaver. That, too, is normal,' said Mr B. 'Where was it you said Mr Curran is staying in Venice?'

She knew she hadn't told him, but she told him now. 'The Lord Byron Hotel. The same as where my husband is staying with the woman.'

'It must be quite an hotel, the Lord Byron,' said Mr B. 'You know, of course, that Byron stayed in Venice where he exercised, if I may say, his human rights.' He took Anthea's hand in one of his, and folded his other hand over it. 'If you decide to depend on me, Mrs Leaver,' he said, 'be sure that you *can* depend on me.'

At nine o'clock that night after trying the Pensione Sofia on the telephone and failing to get Grace, Anthea went about finding the telephone number of the Hotel Lord Byron. She wanted and did not want to talk to Arnold, whoring as he was after strange gods at the Lord Byron, Venice, lush as the Kings of Midian and the chains about their camels' necks … In the heat of his lusts, thought Anthea, I will bust through to his room on the telephone. And so, in process of time he will repent, he will …

When she actually got through to the Lord Byron, she suddenly funked asking for Arnold when she pictured Mary Tiller answering the telephone in the bedroom (which, in Anthea's imagination, was draped in shell-pink satin). After the space of three palpitations, she asked for Curran. To her astonishment she was put through to him right away. 'Excuse me, Mr Curran,' she said timidly, 'you don't know me and I only know you by hearsay as a friend of my son, Robert. I'm Mrs Leaver.'

'Good evening, Mrs Leaver, where are you calling from?'

'I'm speaking from Birmingham where our home is.'

'Ah,' said Curran.

'Do you,' said Anthea, 'have the faintest idea where Robert is?'

'No, I'm afraid I don't,' Curran said. 'He was here in Venice for a few days but he appears to have left.'

'Oh, dear,' said Anthea.

'He left rather suddenly. No doubt he has written to you,' Curran said. 'I'm sorry I can't help you. I'm only here for a few days myself, on business, before returning to the States.'

'I'm sorry to trouble you,' Anthea said, feeling the weight of Curran's objective importance and his unforeseen, casual claim to the overwhelming States. 'I know you've been very kind to Robert in the past,' she said.

'Not at all,' Curran said. 'I shouldn't worry about him, Mrs Leaver, if I were you.'

'Will he return to Paris, do you think?'

'I don't know his plans but if I should bump into him I'll tell him you called.'

'Oh, don't do that. Please, no. He'll think I'm interfering with his life.'

'They do incline to think in that way,' Curran said. 'This must be an expensive call for you, Mrs Leaver. I'm sorry I haven't more information.'

'I'm sorry to have—'

'Not at all. Any time—'

'It was only that my friend Grace Gregory rang me up and she sounded rather funny about Robert. And I hesitate to ask Robert's father, I mean my husband Arnold, because he's supposed to be having a rest ...'

The line had broken down or Curran had hung up. Anthea decided that the former had happened. She told herself, in a panic, that Curran had probably thought she had hung up angrily on her own last words: 'Arnold ... he's supposed to be having a rest'. She dialled again, and again after a while got Curran on the phone.

'I'm sorry, we got cut off,' she said.

Curran said, 'Yes? I thought we had finished the conversation. Is there something else?'

'No. Oh, no. I just wanted to thank you for being so kind to Robert.'

'Not at all. Don't mention it. Goodbye, goodbye.'

'Goodbye, Mr Curran, I'm sorry to—' she said, but he had rung off without waiting for her answer. She bustled about in some fury after that, turned on the television, changed the channel, turned it off, then settled herself down to read her novel: it was a long one but she had almost come to the final chapter. She preferred to read in a chair before going to bed. When she read in bed before going to sleep the novel would lie on her bedside table affecting her dreams so that in a sense, by the morning, she had finished the whole book without actually reading it, and without remembering a word.

Matt, Joyce and Beryl finished their supper in semi-silence, looking enquiringly at each other. Mark, John and Maimie were asleep and only Khorinthia lay awake in her cot looking the image of Beryl as she must have been. The letter from Colin lay open on the table like a time-bomb. Since ever she could remember, Joyce had been waiting for this moment.

At length Matt ventured as he raised his beer-can to his lips, 'This had to happen, I guess.'

The rain poured outside.

Somewhere up the street a car pulled up.

Joyce's arms, rounded and beautiful, were propped on the table. The baby began to cry. Beryl looked at Matt as Joyce got up to attend to Khorinthia.

'It's your choice,' she murmured.

'What choice is there, what choice ever, in the world of today?' he asked violently. Then, drinking his beer, he sighed, 'I could take the job for a limited time ...' He reached for his guitar.

Anthea felt sleepy, but she wanted to read on. She was thinking of making another phone call to Venice. She decided to wait an hour till Grace was sure to have returned to the Pensione Sofia. Sure to be home by midnight ... Anthea fell asleep in her chair. She did not dream of the book but of her grandmother from Scotland who used to chant to her:

> For her I'll dare the billow's roar,
> For her I'll trace a distant shore,
> That Indian wealth may lustre throw
> Around my Highland lassie, O.

13

Tuesday afternoon. Curran had spent the morning with his Italian lawyer who had been summoned overnight from Milan, and even with this old acquaintance Curran had seen the poison of Robert's missive working. The man was plainly uncertain how much Curran had to hide. If there were indeed two halves of a man's body in the garden of the Pensione Sofia, the lawyer pointed out, and should they be exhumed, it might be easy for Curran to deny knowledge of them, but certainly he would be involved in a scandal such as the newspapers of Europe would rejoice in for weeks on end. Yes, said the lawyer, it was true, he was sure, that Curran had not murdered Pancev (imagine it!) but there was no doubt he had known Pancev well ... Then, the question of drugs. Boys and drugs. This is Italy, and you know you would be interrogated. Yes, the young man Leaver would eventually, of course, go to prison for calumny; that was, if he could be found, and if he could be proved to have written these accusations voluntarily. But the publicity would be enormous. On the other hand, if there were not two halves of a body . . .

'I'm afraid there are,' said Curran.

'Then the women are guilty of a crime. Mutilation and concealment of a corpse. Would they accuse you of complicity? And the Countess de Winter?'

'I don't take or traffic in drugs,' was Curran's answer.

The lawyer looked at the pavemented floor of Curran's room in the Hotel Byron where he sat with his client, and smiled wisely.

'The two women at the Pensione Sofia . . . I don't know,' Curran said. 'They might say anything.'

'I tell you,' said the lawyer. 'You're a wealthy American and you have this young man who says he's been kidnapped. Why don't you decide to pay them something? I can arrange for a colleague here in Venice to treat with the kidnappers as soon as we know who they are. They'll be in touch with you, of course. They've calculated your reaction very finely. But you must not inform the police because it's illegal to treat with kidnappers. The magistrate will block the money. In fact this advice I'm giving you is illegal. I just want to help.'

'Thank you,' Curran said. 'I think that's all.'

The lawyer said, 'The young man has written under duress.'

'I don't think so. I think he's joined the gang.'

'What a monster! How did you ever get in the hands of such a youth?'

'It was the dangerous element that I liked, I suppose.

When I met him he was a prostitute on the streets of Paris, posing as a student. As in fact he was, on paper. He has a good mind, too, but ... I always felt the danger. I didn't ... I didn't think ... Oh, well. I'll think over your advice and let you know.'

'Be careful what you say on the telephone. Very careful.'

'I always am.'

The lawyer was in a hurry to leave. It was past two o'clock. Curran wanted to miss lunch; he went for a walk in the cold bright air of the great Piazza, wondering if he, alone, of all the people around him, the sauntering tourists who walked round the arcades and the purposeful Venetians who crossed the square in order to get to the other side, was afflicted with a living nightmare.

He went down to the quay and looked at the scene, with its coffee-table picture charm, along the Riva degli Schiavoni. The gondolas were lined up in wintry abeyance between the mooring-poles; some drivers stood on the landing-stages beside their water-taxis chattering among each other under the shadow of the Doges' Palace, enviably in full charge of their own history. Curran felt an urge to go back to the Lord Byron and wait for a message from Robert's end. It would surely come. He felt an equal urge to avoid the hotel for that very reason. He could not remember a time in his adult life when he had not fully coped with his own life, not to mention the lives of others.

'Curran, I want to speak to you.'

He turned to find Mary Tiller by his side dressed in her mink coat and her tight boots, with her brass-coloured curls

arranged neatly; and yet she looked unusually in disorder, perhaps because her eyes were wider open than usual. 'I want you
to know, Mr Curran, that I'm not a poisoner.'

'You may always call me Curran, Mrs Tiller.'

She relaxed a little and smiled. 'Curran, I am not a poisoner. Whatever Robert has told you, it isn't true. My first
husband died of typhoid in Boulogne; I have the death cer-
tificate. I wasn't there. I—'

'You've had a letter, too, Mary?'

'I have nothing to hide,' she said.

'Don't you?'

'Well, we all have something, I suppose, to hide but—'

'Not necessarily what Robert says it is.'

'Not what he says. That's right. Did he tell you about me,'
Mary said, 'in that letter you got from him at the Pensione
Sofia yesterday? What did he tell you about me?'

'What did he tell you about me?' said Curran.

'I feel embarrassed,' said Mary. 'Has he written like that to
anyone else?'

'Probably quite a few people have received letters from
him,' Curran said. 'The more the better in my opinion. So
that we can know for a fact that he's mad.'

They had started to walk together, back to St Mark's
Square.

'Why do you say that?' she said.

'The wilder his accusations, and the more numerous, the
more easily we can prove him mad.'

'Do you want to prove him mad?'

'Yes.'

Mary said she would like to go into Florian's for tea. On the way across the square she said, 'He told you he was leaving Venice, didn't he?'

'Yes, he did.'

'Don't you think it possible he is still hereabouts? How would he be able to have these letters delivered if he's gone far away?'

'That's a point,' said Curran.

'He must have a friend who's delivering these letters,' Mary said. 'Maybe we're being followed. I feel creepy.'

'So do I,' said Curran.

'You sound as if you mean it.'

They drifted self-consciously into Florian's for tea. They settled in one of the decorative seats with a good view of the entrance.

'You know,' said Mary, 'I don't think Robert's mad. But he might be evil. What's his object?'

'I would like to see the letter he sent you,' said Curran.

'But naturally you won't show me the letter he sent to you,' she said.

'Will you show Arnold his letter?' Curran said.

'My God! You don't think I'd let it be made public, do you?' Mary said. 'It smears my name. All invention of course, except for a few bits here and there – goodness knows how he found out about my affairs. But mud sticks. I couldn't, I really couldn't show anyone that letter.' She spoke haughtily, almost rejecting Curran's friendliness. He could not decide whether she was suspicious of him for some reason, or whether she was simply frightened.

'Mary, are you suspicious of me for some reason?' he said.

'Why should I be?'

'What did Robert say about me in his letter?'

'I wouldn't repeat it,' she said.

'But you don't know if it's true or not? This is a very unnerving situation.'

'Robert has foreseen that, I think. Robert must have had this in mind for at least a couple of years,' she said, 'because before that he didn't know of my existence. Since then, he must have been collecting information, snooping into my life, distorting it, and now these inventions. When I think of how I went round Venice yesterday so worried about him . . . Well, I'm going to tear up the letter and forget it. We shouldn't even discuss Robert; he's not worth it.'

'That's true. But we are also trying to protect ourselves, aren't we?'

'You may be,' she said.

'The best way would be to go to the police. Do you have the courage? We should all have the courage—'

'I would sue when I got home to England, I really would.'

'You might have to sue here. It's an offence committed on this territory.'

She said, 'I have to think of Arnold, don't I? He thinks the world of his good name and he's terrified of his wife Anthea.'

'It might be good for Arnold,' said Curran, 'if he, too, got a letter from Robert.'

'He's under the impression that Robert's gone back to Paris. He said last week he didn't think Robert would ever stay here and write his thesis on that church.'

'The Santa Maria Formosa?' As Curran said this it occurred to him that this church might well be a focus-point for contact with Robert. Robert had been studying the architecture; he had been seen in the church and outside it the day he disappeared.

Curran now lost interest in Mary but waited politely till she had finished her tea. He walked back with her to the Lord Byron hotel. There were no messages for him. He phoned Violet. 'Any message for me?' 'No.' 'Thanks. See you later.' He then set out for the Pensione Sofia by way of the Campo di Santa Maria Formosa. He found himself looking at the passing faces, suspiciously, so that they looked back with enquiry and suspicion, too.

As he walked, he went over in his mind the meeting with his lawyer that morning: '... the women are guilty of a crime. Mutilation and concealment of a corpse. Would they, would the Countess de Winter, accuse you of complicity?'

I will of course leave Venice, he thought. I'll get out, and quick. But, as if his lawyer himself were arguing the point, he argued with himself. To leave would go against me. Where could I go that a scandal wouldn't touch me? I'm not a Nobody. Even if I were a Nobody ... And besides, he thought, I would like to see Robert. I would like to see him just once more and tell him what I think of him.

Lina Pancev had spent Tuesday morning in bed recovering from her plunge into the canal the night before. Violet's doctor had given her some antibiotics to take against a possible infection from the canal waters wherein she had tried to cleanse herself from the contamination of Leo. Hugely intrigued by the affair, Leo had come to see her in the middle of the morning.

Violet had gone out, having told Lina firmly that she would not be back for lunch; which meant Lina was meant to get up and get her own lunch. This was already one cause for indignation, for Lina felt she had a right to be looked after. Her indignation at finding out that Leo was a Jew in her bed had been largely exorcised by her dive into the canal, and by the time Leo turned up to visit her, had subsided back into the amorphous mass of half-conscious prejudices that had so far propelled her through her life.

Leo brought up a letter for her from the hall table directed from her old attic address in Venice, and she read it while he made coffee on the spirit-stove. She was not listening to what he was saying at all, but he was telling her how funny she was in general despite the fact that she was a rotten sleep, too excitable. She caught the last word 'excitable'. She said, 'You would be excitable, too, if you got a letter like this.' She started to cry. 'I'm having a terrible time, and now I'm losing my refugee grant,' she said, taking her coffee from Leo's hands.

The letter was from a woman-friend in Paris, forewarning her of a more official letter to come.

The Group feels this way. Don't be upset, Lina, but you know you never answer letters, sign petitions or come to our meetings and our demonstrations. Additional to this, there has been a report that you are not seriously a

Dissident. Isn't it true, Lina, that you believe in nothing and know nothing of our struggle? Please do not take this personally, but you should never have left Bulgaria. Nobody was persecuting you. You do not suffer. You do not share our aims. Many stories have been whispered about you. Your ideas ...

Leo listened while she read it out. 'Let them keep their money. You've got a job,' he said.

'I've got enemies,' Lina said. 'All round me, I've got enemies. I don't know what to do.'

'You could get up and go to the movies this afternoon. I've got to go now. I've got to meet Grace.'

'Nobody cares about me. Even Robert has gone away, I don't know where.'

'See you,' said Leo, and left.

Lina got up, feeling sick from her antibiotics and her bad news. She got dressed with the one aim in mind of buying a train ticket for Paris so that she could go there and confront her enemies and save her allowance from the fund.

When she came down to the ground floor in the lift, Violet's cleaning woman was there, just about to leave. She pointed with a glowing smile to the hall table where a wrapping of cellophane enclosed a bunch of flowers which, as Lina peered closer, turned out to be small, fresh roses of various colours, addressed to her. The offering had a decidedly shop-bought look although the label itself was home-made cut-out with a typed address.

'Who sent these?' Lina enquired of the woman who stood

there marvelling, crowing her envy and hopping with curiosity.

'They were left outside the door. Your admirer didn't even ring the bell. I found them on the step. They must have thrown them out of a passing boat for you, because no one stopped in a boat at the landing-stage; nothing passed, no delivery, all morning. You must have a *cavaliere*.'

'You must be a fool,' said Lina in the frustration of the morning's news, the antibiotics and excitement of the moment. She tore at the cellophane. The woman reacted with proper indignation. '*Cavaliere!*' said Lina. 'Who has horses in Venice to ride to the door?' This rude reasoning was lost on the woman, who said it was only a manner of speaking and enquired sanely if Lina didn't feel so well.

But Lina had found a small envelope tucked into the flowers. Inside she found a card on which was typed:

Be at the Hotel Lord Byron in the lounge this afternoon (Tues.) from 2.30 onwards and await a phone call. You will be paged. Tell nobody repeat nobody.

ROBERT

Lina drew her thick brown shawl round about her shoulders, put the card in her bulky bag and walked out, lifting her skirts above the very slippery side-path till she came to the corner of the Ca' Winter and, watched by the scornful cleaning woman, disappeared about her business. The woman took the flowers into Violet's apartment, put them in water and purged the entrance hall of its cellophane, green twine and the mess of little leaves that had detached themselves from the bunch.

At two o'clock, having had a glass of beer and a pizza, Lina was in the hall of the Hotel Lord Byron, urging upon the reception clerk her claim to be called from the lounge the moment a call came through for her. The clerk, looking at Lina's unprosperous clothes, was tentatively obstructive; he did not want to provoke a possible student protest, as might well happen these days by refusing to take a call for someone who looked like Lina; at the same time, she looked unlikely to give him a tip, had made no move to do so, and besides, the reputation of the hotel had to be kept up. He muttered something about the manager's orders. He said he had no authority to put through calls to anybody but clients of the hotel.

'Do you realise,' said Lina, 'who I am? Call the manager. My father was once a regular patron of this hotel.' She felt sure this was true, and anyway, it worked. The clerk agreed to leave her name with the telephone operator and to inform her when and if her call came through. He indicated a darkish corner of the lobby where she could wait. He suggested she order something to drink in the meantime, or even a coffee. On enquiring the price of a coffee at the Lord Byron, Lina declined this suggestion. She took herself off to her corner table, snatching up a glossy magazine from another table on the way.

It was at about two-thirty that Arnold Leaver came up to her. He said, 'Good afternoon, windy, isn't it?'

'Oh, Professor Leaver, good afternoon.'

'I'm not a professor. As a matter of fact, I'm entitled to doctor but you realize in England only a medico uses "doctor". May I take a chair? That's why nobody else *wants* to be "doctor" in England, is my belief. The profession has gone down, down, down.'

He put on an expression of expectant gloom as if waiting for her to cap his statement with something worse. He had a brown woollen scarf tied round his neck although the hotel was centrally heated. He wore a rough but not old brown tweed jacket with leather patches at the elbows and well-pressed grey flannel trousers. To Lina, all this was a comforting sign; his neatness, his little yellow moustache, his seemly old-fashioned spectacles, the big freckle-marks on his hairy hands, and his well-kept finger-nails took her back to her safe childhood, probably reminding her of some good, sound uncle. She told him she had seen a Venetian doctor the night before, having slipped into the canal, and that the doctor had given her antibiotics. 'They make me feel awful,' she said.

'He must be a criminal,' said Arnold. 'What have antibiotics to do with a drenching? I should have said an aspirin with hot lemon.'

'Well, the canal water is infectious.'

'What rot!' said Arnold. 'Doctors and their antibiotics. Fortunately I have a doctor in England who knows his job. No nonsense about him. He was the school doctor when I was head of Ambrose, and that's why he knows what's what. He ordered me to take this holiday. That's why I'm taking it. And he gave a strong recommendation that I should come without my wife Anthea.' He was looking intently into Lina's face as he spoke. Antibiotics and canal water regardless she looked in the best of health and no man, he noted, who could call himself a man could fail to appreciate that she was a bright-eyed, a full-fledged and juicy young woman. 'My wife Anthea,' he said, 'threatened to sue the doctor. Just imagine . . . We've never been separated before, all our married life. My wife Anthea is a great anxiety to me, my dear. Anything the matter?'

She had half-risen in her chair because from where they were sitting the ring of the incoming telephone calls could be faintly heard, and apparently one of these calls was for somebody for whom the desk clerk was now looking round the lobby. From afar he noticed Lina's movement, but shook his head when she pointed to her chest and formed the words 'For me?' Lina sat down again. 'I'm sorry,' she said, 'but I'm waiting for a definite call. You were telling me about your wife. You know it is all right for you to enjoy your holiday without a wife, but Mrs Tiller should not have come with you.'

'In a way,' he said, 'you're right. In another way, you're wrong. When a man is in need of a change, a cheerful *and* generous companion like Mary Tiller is not to be sneezed at.'

'Oh, I didn't mean to suggest one should always sneeze or spit over a woman who takes to her bed a married man,' said Lina. 'But I can also see the point of view of the good and faded wife. In my country where I come from, there is two points of view, and we are taught to look upon both of them.'

'We, too, attempt to see the other side, objectively,' said Arnold. 'So you and I have a point in common, there.

However, I must say, my holiday so far has been a disappointment on the whole.'

A waiter now put in an appearance, needlessly shifting ash-trays and the small flower-vases on the other tables nearby. 'Can I offer you a drink?' said Arnold to bright-cheeked Lina.

'I'll have a cup of coffee, thanks.'

'One coffee, one whisky and soda *no* ice,' Arnold said to the waiter. 'First,' he said to Lina, 'there is the problem of my wife Anthea in Birmingham very discontented about my holiday, and second, who should I meet when I set foot in Venice but my son, Robert. Let me tell you at once, my dear, that I know you're a friend of Robert's. I don't want to spoil anything between you. But I must say, speaking for myself, that I was very glad indeed when I heard that Robert had left Venice. I hope he's gone back to Paris to his studies, but his gentleman-friend, gentleman so-called, Curran is still here.'

Lina wanted very much to tell Arnold about the message that had come with the roses. But she remembered that she was to 'tell nobody' and was intrigued by the mystery of the phone call to come, and decided to wait, even though she was annoyed that the message had come at second-hand.

She said, 'Robert should have told me he was going away. He should get in touch with me. He owes it to me. He was to have helped me to move my belongings when I moved into my new job.'

'If you're thinking that my son is reliable,' said Arnold, 'my dear, you can think again. I say no more.' His whisky and her coffee arrived. He drank his whisky quickly while she was still stirring her coffee, and ordered another. He said to Lina, 'Mary Tiller is a fine woman but she's bossy. Today she was in a terrible state, I don't know why. She went off immediately after lunch, on her own. Not much company for me, you know. I'm supposed to be on holiday. If she can go off on her own, then I can go off on my own. What are you doing tonight, my dear? Would you like to dine with me at some restaurant of your choice?'

Lina thought that would be the loveliest thing in the world and said so. She half-expected that the phone call she was awaiting would be from Robert himself, telling her he was returning to Venice. It would be good for him if she had another date. Especially with Robert's father.

Arnold's second whisky arrived at the same time as Lina was called to the telephone. She took it in the box she was ushered to. A woman spoke. She sounded young.

'Miss Lina Pancev?'

'Yes.'

'I have a message for you from Robert Leaver.'

'Where is Robert?' she said. 'Who are you?'

'I'm a friend of Robert. Robert is not here at present. You are to tell nobody. Robert is in difficulties. It is not possible for you to see him. Tell nobody. Be in the garden of the Pensione Sofia at midnight tonight. Be in the garden. You can enter by the gate at the garden entrance. If you have any difficulty you can climb over. Then keep close to the wall at the side of the Rio.'

'Rio? What—'

'The side-canal. Keep close to the wall. You will receive a

message there from Robert. Tell nobody. Robert wants you to do this for him. You are in no danger.'

'Where's Robert?'

'Robert wants you to be there, for him.'

'Will I see Robert tonight?'

'No. He will see you. At midnight in the garden of the Pensione Sofia you will have a message.'

'I'd be afraid to do that. What's the mystery?'

'Tell nobody.' The woman rang off.

Lina went off to the ladies' room before returning to Arnold. She felt sure Robert was mocking her, somewhere. She was furious with Robert for sending messages through other people, and especially through this young woman with her officious tone.

When she got back to Arnold she said, 'Well, that's that job done. When will you call for me tonight?'

At the Pensione Sofia Curran said, 'Still no message?'

'Half an hour ago,' said Katerina, sulkily, 'a certain man rang up. He said, "Did Curran get the message?" I said, "Who's speaking?" He said, "Tell Curran he's got a week to act." That's all. He hung up.'

'Did you recognize the voice?' Curran said.

'How could I not recognize the voice when we've been paying that voice all these years. The Butcher's assistant who's become the Butcher since his master died. It can't be anyone else, can it?'

They were in the small office that led from the hall. Eufemia came in. 'We've just heard from the Butcher,' she said.

'I was telling him about it,' Katerina said.

Eufemia said to Curran, 'What are you going to do about it?'

'Why me?' Curran said. 'What has it got to do with me?'

'Well, didn't you kill Pancev?' said Eufemia.

'No. And you know I didn't.'

Katerina said, 'Nothing would have happened after all these years if it were not for you and your money and your boy. It's your money they're after, that's all.'

'I know,' said Curran.

'Well, give them the money and let us remain in peace.'

'With your man cut in two in the garden,' Curran said.

'Now we can see the mean side of him,' Katerina said to Eufemia. 'Always so courteous, so condescending. Now he's going to turn on us rather than pay.'

'Really, we should stick together,' Curran said. 'It's a moral issue. We need courage.'

'You'll need more courage than we do,' said Eufemia. 'How do we know you didn't kill Pancev?'

'You know quite well,' Curran said, and hurriedly left the place.

Violet, he thought, is the only friend I can share this trouble with. She's the only person I can count on. It was getting on for evening as he turned into the square of the Santa Maria Formosa. The church was closed. He walked all round it, then suddenly saw the man he was looking for. He recognized, sure enough, the middle-aged man who, with the young woman, had been following Robert and Lina, and who Curran had imagined was some foreign agent trailing Lina.

174

That had been, in fact, when Curran had himself followed the young people about Venice, obsessed as to what his Robert was doing with the girl.

Now, the man, stocky and bald, standing at the side entrance to the church, simply stared at Curran. The man wore a dark blue windjammer. He looked poor in his dress, but his expression was sophisticated, not that of a poor man. He looked at Curran as if the look alone were a message. Curran looked away and walked on into the dusk, increasing his pace as he walked, making up his mind to acquire a gun to protect himself. The newspapers of Italy were fed by continual kidnappings. Curran thought: Why should I be spared? And he thought again, as he made his way across the bridges and down the small alleys, to Violet's house: If this were a dream, then I would wake abruptly with fear. But it isn't a dream. A water-taxi arrived at Violet's landing-stage as Curran came round the narrow footpath that led to it from the streets behind the house. In the lamplight Curran saw a stout, youngish man coming down the steps from the hall and as he entered the motor-boat the man looked at Curran with a smile. Curran didn't recognize him at all. But then he noticed the man was smiling at the driver and smiling to himself, and, in fact, it was a built-in expression that Curran had noticed, not a smile at all.

Arnold sat opposite Lina at nine o'clock that night at Harry's Bar. He felt great satisfaction. Mary had put up no opposition to his going out to dine 'on his own'; in fact, she had positively encouraged him to do so; she wanted an early night herself, she had said, for she felt a cold coming on. Now, Lina, with a snow-white shawl replacing her everyday brown one, was proving to be an excellent companion. He had already told her that he gave her full marks, and as she had misunderstood this compliment – 'What kind of a mark? A mark on my face?' – he had exuberantly explained that she went to the top of the class. 'Like Mary Tiller?' she said.

'Well I give Mary six out of ten.'

He then pointed out that Lina herself got ten out of ten, for which she thanked him, and she toasted him in the last of the champagne.

Arnold said, 'I bet you can't spell "psychedelic".'

To his amazement and joy she not only could spell it but she knew what it meant. He ordered another bottle of champagne.

Lina told him about the impending loss of her grant from the refugee fund: '. . . because they say I don't suffer and fight. Those dissidents who stay at home are the ones who suffer. What have we got to suffer about?'

He quite agreed. He unburdened himself on the subject of his wife Anthea until Lina announced that it was past eleven.

'Must you go home so early?' Arnold said.

'Not at all,' said Lina, and made up her mind triumphantly to a course of action which had been struggling in her thoughts since she had received that telephone message from the unknown woman and those roses with that message also at second hand. She was now full of champagne and courage as she said, 'I have an idea!'

'Let's hear it,' he said, hopefully.

'We'll go for a walk in a garden by moonlight. It's a

beautiful, clear night and we're alone in Venice, the two of us.'

'A garden? Won't that be rather chilly?'

She sipped her champagne. 'If it's chilly, Arnold, we'll run, we'll dance.'

She laughed a lot as he paid the bill, which itself for a few moments spoiled the smile on Arnold's face, he being unused to the going rate for champagne at the best restaurants. However, he paid with a half-smile which, when that was done, soon turned eager again.

'It's years,' he said, 'and years, my dear, since I walked with a lovely lady in a garden. Where is this garden of yours? Is it near your home? Perhaps, afterwards, we could slip indoors . . .'

To cool him down a little, as they walked through the alleys she told him the sad story of her father's death and burial in Venice all those years ago, and how she had looked in vain for his grave. At last they came to the wall that ran along beside the Pensione Sofia, with the canal gleaming by its side. She led him along the footpath till they came to the wooden side-gate. 'Here's the garden,' she said.

The gate was locked. She lifted her skirts and started to climb over. 'This is the Pensione Sofia, isn't it?' said Arnold.

'That's right. Don't worry. The two old ladies have gone to bed. It's nearly midnight.' She landed on the other side of the gate. 'Come on,' she said.

'I wonder if my old bones can manage . . .' He managed fairly well with the steadying help of her hand. Someone shouted from a barge. Arnold started and looked guiltily over the gate towards the shouter but the shout was evidently meant to carry up the canal to another barge which returned the unintelligible cry.

'How lovely it is here. Look at the roses,' Lina said. She was walking up the path towards the dark house with its shuttered windows. Only a few of the guests were still up, faint creaks of light showing between their shutters. The ground floor was in darkness except for a dim light penetrating the back of the long room from the porter's place.

'We're quite alone,' said Lina, pulling her white shawl about her. The sound of a paddle from a rowing-boat or gondola came from the canal, as if approaching the gate.

Arnold said, 'This is quite an adventure, I must say.' He had an overcoat buttoned up. He sniffed in the chilly air and looked up at the stars.

'I wonder,' said Lina, 'if there's anyone watching us from the house.' She ran down the path to peer in through the ironwork which protected the large glass door into the house. Arnold followed her. The night porter could not be seen; only the dim light from his room.

They set off again down the path. Suddenly Lina said, 'Quiet! I can hear someone coming by the canal. Perhaps they're coming home to the Pensione by the back gate.'

She ran to the wall beside the water-gate, leaving Arnold on the path. The boat paddled gently in to the side of the canal and stopped. 'Are you there?' said a woman's voice in Italian. She answered, in Italian, 'Yes, it's me, Lina.'

'But you're not alone.'

'No. Why should I be? I've got my man with me.'

The voice said, 'Your friend wants you to dance for him.

He wants you to dance in those centre rose-beds, the special enclosed ones. Dance on the far one and then on the near one.'

'Where is *Roberto?*'

'Not far away.'

'I want to speak to him.'

She jumped to see over the wall.

She saw a long heavy boat with a makeshift tarpaulin hood at the prow under which someone darkly disappeared with a scurry as Lina's head bobbed up. A woman in dark trousers with long blonde hair was bending to rest one of the oars. Lina went to the gate to have a better look, but this time the woman was sitting in the boat with a scarf over the lower part of her face.

'Do as he says,' the woman muttered from under the scarf, in a way that sounded as if she were impatient with the business.

'All right. I'll dance with my man-friend,' Lina said out loud.

By this time Arnold was beside her, peering at the boat, unable to follow this exchange of Italian. 'What's going on?' he said. 'Are they guests at the Pensione?'

'No, they're just nobodies,' she said. 'They're looking for somewhere to tie up their boat.' She took his hand and started to guide him back to the path.

'What are they going to do?'

'What do you think?' said Lina. 'Forget them.' She started to skip. 'Do you know, I feel cold and you look cold, Arnold. I'm going to dance. Let's dance together.'

She jumped right into the nearest hooped enclosure and swung her white shawl wide. 'Dance?' he said. 'Oh, dear,' he said. But he laughed with delight and stepped over the railing into the magic rose-bed ring. All round the rose-bed they tripped, she flapping her shawl while Arnold took off his scarf and waved it wildly in the air. They jumped a sort of polka-step hand-in-hand, all round the grass surrounding the roses. 'Now the other side of the path, their other private rose-bed,' Lina commanded. 'It's fun. Only you and I. The two old women will never know.' She had seen two figures at the landing-stage, crouching, peering through the gate.

Arnold leapt after her to the other rose-bed. 'What does it matter,' she cried in Italian, 'who sees us?'

'My dear, I don't follow your Italian. You talk so fluently and I'm slow. But I tell you I'm having the time of my life. Sorry if I'm a bit breathless.'

She began to sing a song in another language strange to him, probably Bulgarian, and danced by herself with her white shawl flying. Arnold followed as best he could. 'Hooray!' he cried.

The oars by the water-gate began to splash. Lina stopped to listen and put out her hand to stop Arnold, too. 'It's only that couple going away,' she said.

From the canal came a burst of a man's laughter. It was a convulsed sound. Then the effort of rowing must have overtaken the man, for his laugh became intermittent as the boat receded down the canal. A woman's laughter mingled with the man's, in the distance, before the boat turned the corner.

Lina, too, was laughing, standing on the path, pulling her shawl about her. And Arnold laughed with her.

'Those people must have watched us,' Lina said, and laughed again at the thought.

He said, 'As well they don't know us, isn't it? Well, that was a Venetian adventure, my dear you've made my holiday. Golly! As well my wife Anthea can't see us.' And he laughed to himself as one who, having been cheated of many things, has in some small way recuperated his loss.

14

'His name is B.,' said Violet, 'so far as I've ever known or, I suppose, ever will know. The organization, as you know, is called GESS which stands for Global-Equip Security Services.'

'But you sent for him,' said Curran.

'No, I did not.'

'I can't believe that you did not.'

'Believe or not believe,' said Violet. 'He was annoyed, in fact, that I had not sent for him. I didn't tell you at the time; it wasn't important. I had one little job to do: investigate Arnold Leaver and Mary Tiller. When I found out that it was a perfectly banal affair with no prospects I sent back a message to GESS saying just that. I didn't mention you; I had no reason to. He thinks I should have done.'

'Mention me? Why?'

'Because you were connected with Arnold Leaver's son and you are rich, and I knew it.'

'Violet, I don't know if I can trust you. What brought him here?'

'He heard from someone else that you were involved with Robert and that Robert's missing. Word gets round.'

'What is he here for? What's his purpose?'

'Business.'

'Violet, you have a sinister side and I've always known it. You mean, blackmail.'

'Persuasion,' she said, 'is the phrase he prefers.'

'Does he know what Robert's doing to us? Does he know where Robert is?'

'Yes, he does,' she said.

'My God! How did he find that out?'

'I told him,' Violet said. 'And I want you to understand that I've acted for the best. GESS are professionals, whereas Robert and the Butcher are amateurs. B. of GESS can put them in their place. He can give us immunity at bargain price.'

'It's a trick,' Curran said. 'I hate being a wealthy man; I hate it.'

'Easily remedied,' Violet said.

'I suggest,' said Curran, 'that you start first. Give away your palazzo. Give away your jewellery. Give—'

'What palazzo? What jewellery? I'm nothing but a landlady and my jewellery's in pawn for safekeeping.'

'Pay Mr B. of GESS the bargain price yourself,' Curran said. 'Why should I pay?'

'Sooner or later,' she said, 'you're going to be kidnapped.'

'Here in Venice, it wouldn't be easy.'

'But somewhere else in the world—'

'Not necessarily,' he said. 'I don't have regular habits. I'm here, I'm there and I'm everywhere. It's the people with regular habits who generally get taken.'

'You don't have bodyguards.'

'Bodyguards are a kind of prison. I find this conversation distasteful.'

'And me,' said Violet. 'It's as if we've fallen into a calculated trap.'

'It's exactly,' he said, 'as if Robert had planned our reactions.'

'Don't you detest Robert?' she said.

'Perhaps I always did,' he said.

'But he's surprised you.'

'Yes. Oh, yes. He's more interesting than I thought. From the objective point of view I'd rather read those notes and letters of his than listen to his wild ideas for theses that he never got down to. I've listened for two years, one after the other. From the objective point of view—'

'How I envy,' she said, 'your being rich enough to take an objective point of view in a case where you're involved.'

'It's only because of my money that I'm involved in the first place,' he said. 'And, I have to admit, it's only because of my money that you are involved, and Mary Tiller—'

'That's why,' she said, 'I confided in B. of GESS. I did it on impulse, and I'm glad. I was stunned when he called here this evening; he had just arrived in Venice and came straight here.'

'He questioned you about me.'

'Oh, yes. He knows all about you. He seems to know your very banking secrets. Maybe he doesn't know everything, but he seems to. He was resentful I hadn't told him before that I know you.'

'I hope that's true,' he said.

'It is true. I didn't bring him here. Anyway, I told him about our present difficulties. He can settle the matter for half a million. That gives you immunity for now and the future, according to him.'

This made Curran laugh, to her relief. 'And the future . . .' he said. Something about the phrase amused him greatly, so that she said, 'I know he can't guarantee anyone's safety for the future. I'm just telling you what he said.'

'How is he going to stop the Butcher's gang?'

'Is it a gang?'

'I really don't know. So how can your friend B. know?'

'He's not my friend. But I've got confidence in him. GESS are organized. They can get in touch with anyone if the job's big enough, any territory in the world. They can tap telephones; they can hide radiation devices in umbrellas, coat buttons, tooth stoppings; they can bribe the filing clerks and photocopy computer information; they—'

'You mean persuade the clerks,' said Curran.

'I mean persuade.'

'And half a million dollars will be final?' Curran said.

'He thinks so, Curran. Relatively speaking, B. of GESS is a godsend. I'd rather deal with a professional businessman, honestly I would, than a gang of evil amateurs. Wouldn't you?'

Tuesday night came to an end as Curran agreed. He stayed with Violet another hour, refusing to talk about the business, and wondering very much why he still admired her.

Wednesday morning.

'May I speak to Mr B.?' said Anthea, having telephoned to the GESS office at Coventry.

'Mr B. is away from the office. Who is speaking?'

The GESS pamphlet which she had picked up to get the telephone number, trembled in her hand. 'It's Mrs Leaver, one of his clients. When will Mr B. return?'

'Mr B. is abroad for a few days. Can I take a message?'

'I wanted to say I've thought over the matter and I don't want to proceed.'

'Very well,' said the girl. 'I'll give Mr B.—'

'You see,' said Anthea, 'it's a question of my son's privacy. I don't want—'

'We prefer not to discuss details on the phone. I'll give Mr B. your message.'

The girl had hung up. Anthea looked at the trembling folder in her hand. She felt deprived of Mr B. The folder was looking worn from use. Anthea opened it flat, yet once more. Missing persons . . . Backgrounds checked . . . But for 'backgrounds' she first misread 'blackguards'; it was a dark overclouded morning and very little daylight penetrated the sitting-room. She put up her hand to switch on the standard lamp by her side and it glowed under its silk-fringed shade. Fidelity Department . . . Bureau of Ethics and Charisma . . .

The telephone rang. It was a married woman-friend wondering if she were free for dinner that evening. Anthea lost her friend for ever by snapping that she was never free for dinner without a week's warning.

Lina Pancev, the day after the night she danced on her father's grave, all unknowingly then and indeed for ever, felt she had effectively put Robert in his place by dancing at his bidding, but with his father. She had recognized Robert's laugh and taken it for bravado in front of his new girl-friend.

Lina had connected his disappearance from her life only vaguely with his discovering that Arnold was in Venice with Mary Tiller, his disagreement with Curran ('I told him to go to hell') and possibly some jealousy of Leo. She felt she had been badly used by Robert. He had sent her messages, flowers, indirectly and in the third person, using his new girl, had tried to make her into a dancing exhibition at his bidding. That she had taken his father along to the midnight show at the Pensione Sofia gave her a lively sense of justice having been done.

Violet had suddenly told her not to go shopping at that special butcher any more; this upset Lina because she counted this butcher, Giorgio, as a friend of hers. She had found Giorgio's shop in a crumbling building, overhung with brave geraniums, in a poor part of Venice. He had given her cheap cuts of meat for stew, and had saved up that lard for her which she set much store by. Now, Violet, who had at first been delighted when Lina had undertaken to do the shopping economically, had warned Lina off her butcher. And seeing Lina's resistance, Violet had declared a Month of Vegetarianism for the Ca' Winter.

'You can't impose the vegetarian on me,' Lina said. 'I'm entitled to my meals as I want them if I work for you.'

Violet had seemed to Lina to be rather sick-looking in the past few days, and Lina told her so, ignoring Violet's rage. 'What do you mean,' Lina said, 'that I have to leave the job with you? I have my rights to my job and my bed and my food, or you pay me big compensation. You better buy meat for my supper. For lunch, I am invited out to the Hotel Lord Byron.'

As she left the house there arrived by water-taxi a man with a smiling face. He seemed to be smiling at Lina and she stopped on the footpath before putting up her umbrella against the heavy rain. She looked at him to see if she recognized him, but it seemed he was not smiling at her at all, for he went right into the hall and went up the stairs to Violet's flat. Lina then assumed that he was one of Violet's lovers, put up her umbrella, and went her way along the narrow pathway, round the corner, and into the criss-cross of streets under the pelting rain. It was ten o'clock in the morning. She was due at the Lord Byron to lunch with Arnold Leaver at one o'clock. She decided that having prepared the breakfast and put the dishes, including those from Violet's supper last night, into the dishwasher she would take the rest of the daylight hours to herself. Let Violet do her own vegetarian shopping. On a day and in a place so very watery, after the excitement of last night's triumph-dance among the roses followed by a brief sleep and then the clearing away of dishes in Violet's greyish kitchen, Lina worked herself up as she plodded, against the suggestion of a vegetarian *au pair* job. She went into the Academy to look at some pictures, and indulged her mood by reflecting that there were just as good in Bulgaria's museums. She slopped over the great square to St Mark's to look at the mosaics and actually said out loud, in English, to a group of five ardent Americans, 'We have also in Bulgaria.' The Americans, three men and two women, responded only by moving closer together so that individually they were more like limbs of the one body than they were before.

Lina wanted a coffee but she grudged paying the money at a bar seeing that she was entitled to her morning coffee at home. She recalled that her lodger, the Ethiopian student, who had paid her three months' rent in advance, had also, while handing over the money, thrown in a friendly invitation to come and visit him whenever she wanted. He had given her a grand smile such as only people who have nothing to lose and nothing to gain can give away; at the time she had felt a slight envy for that spontaneous flash of huge yellow-white teeth in the darkness of his face, and the sheer largesse which her lodger was capable of scattering so easily, with only a smile. Lina went off, heading among the puddles, to her old eyrie, telling herself righteously that she ought to see how her tenant was treating her flat.

'Do you mind if I come in for a few moments?' she said, walking into the room. She was delighted to find her tenant at home; obviously he had not long got out of bed. He wore only his trousers and he turned to rummage among the bedclothes for his woollen pullover after he had opened the door. Now Lina saw there was another man sitting in the room, dark and thin-faced. He was biting into a pear. The image of Serge, her second cousin, her Bulgarian companion of past years who had put all the ideas of foreign travel into her head, now jumped before her eyes and was gone; she looked closer as he smiled, sitting with the pear in his hand. He not only looked like Serge, he was Serge.

'What are you doing here?' Lina said, weakly.

'I'm looking for you.'

The Ethiopian said, 'He came here last night so I made him sleep here. Another has been looking for you. Your landlord, he wants his rent. I told him you had rent from me and he was angry. Did I say the right thing, the wrong thing?' He always communicated in English with an American inflection, this being his second language.

'You can have your rent money back,' Lina said. 'Serge, tell this man he has to go away. This is my room.'

Serge took a final bite of the pear and placed the core on a saucer, took out a packet of cigarettes, offered one to the Ethiopian and took one himself. 'Nowhere to go,' said the Ethiopian.

'Go back to your own country,' Lina said.

'Who, me?' said Serge.

'No, him.'

'Have you read the newspapers?' said the Ethiopian student. 'What home, what country?'

Serge said, 'I know her. She doesn't mean these things. She's got a shock to see me, that's all.'

'How did you get into this country?' Lina said to Serge in Bulgarian.

'By tourist visa,' he said in the same language. The Ethiopian looked downcast.

Serge looked round the room. She had left behind some of her drawings and paintings when she had moved to Violet's. He pointed to a painting which was propped against the wall. 'That's your new work?' he said, continuing their Bulgarian conversation. 'Venetian fishermen?'

'Of course not. Those are men fishing by a bridge in Paris.'

'They look too prosperous and contented,' Serge said. 'In the West, the proletariat are not like that. You are painting propaganda.'

'You've come to spy on me,' Lina said, crying.

'No, I've come to take you back. It will be quite all right, no unpleasantness. I've arranged everything. I have a very good job.'

The Ethiopian was putting on his shoes. 'You like me to leave you alone some hours?' he said.

'Certainly not,' Lina said. 'I have a date for lunch with a gentleman. Thank you very much.'

'Anthea, this is Grace. So glad to catch you in. I want to tell you that Mary Tiller moved out of the Hotel Lord Byron this morning. She's moved back to my Pensione. There's been a complete break with Arnold for some reason. I told you it wouldn't last. Leave it to Grace.'

'How did you manage it, Grace?' said Anthea.

'Well, it largely managed itself. I think Mary began to get scared for some reason.'

'Scared?'

'Of her reputation and so forth.'

'She should have thought of that in the first place.'

'Too true. Anyway I said to her, "Mary, you take my advice and come over to my Pensione. There's more going on there."'

'Is Arnold coming home, then?'

'Oh, well, of course, I can't tell you that. He's taken a paternal interest in a foreign girl student, but only paternal. I only know what I see. I told you Mary Tiller's a nice woman at heart. You would like her, really you would, Anthea, if you only got to know her.'

'Should I ring up Arnold?' Anthea said. 'Poor man, all on his own there in Italy. The things I read about Italy.'

'I wouldn't run after him if I were you,' Grace said. 'Let him realize where his bread's buttered.'

'Has Robert come back to Venice?' Anthea said.

'No sign of him, and a good thing too. He only upsets the apple-cart; though he's your son, Anthea, I have to say it.'

'That Mr Curran still around?' Anthea said.

'Oh, yes. Curran's a very nice person, really.

'I don't deny it,' Anthea said. 'He was a good friend to Robert, giving him free digs and all that. I didn't ever tell Arnold because he's got such a suspicious mind. As if he didn't know his own son, as I do. But if you ask me, I'm sure Robert will be glad to go back to Paris to Curran's flat. Grace, you know, I'm only trying to piece together the picture.'

'Why don't you come here yourself?' Grace said.

'Oh, I couldn't do that. There's the fish and so on.' Anthea looked at the goldfish as she spoke, darting round the fresh, bright bowl that fitted in with every other shiny and spotless thing in the living-room. 'Let me know, Grace,' she said, 'as soon as you hear word of Robert.'

'I only came to sort out Arnold,' Grace said. 'My competence doesn't range beyond that. And now he's parted from poor Mary Tiller I feel I should enjoy myself. It's as much as I can do to keep my eye on Leo. But of course if Robert turns up I'll tell him to write to you. I'll tell him in no uncertain terms. I saw some mosaic pictures this afternoon. Mary Tiller and I latched on to a group so we got a guided tour. The guide was a lovely English gentleman of the old school. He brought things to your notice, like "note the ineffable beauty of the dark blues and the golds"—'

At this point the line broke down.

15

On the Thursday afternoon when Robert left the scene he entered his hiding-place with only a little apprehension that he might be walking into a trap. The idea, 'walking into a trap', had been very much in his mind since he had struck up a remarkable friendship with the middle-aged man and the young woman who had been so much in evidence, since Robert arrived in Venice, as to suggest they were positively following him. Or following him, perhaps, with an eye to Lina? Or to Curran? They were certainly not tourists. Robert had noticed them almost from the time Curran caught up with him in Venice. Curran had said, 'Lina's being followed.' It was difficult to be sure. Robert tried to put this strange couple to the test in his movements by day and night. Further down the Grand Canal, turn to the right, cross the little bridge, take the path facing you in the opposite direction, along the side-path of a narrow canal, cross another bridge:

wherever he came out, somehow, ahead of him or approaching him, were the same middle-aged man with a windjammer and dark grey trousers and a girl with long fair hair, a thick woollen jersey and jeans.

It was a week before that Thursday when he went off with them that Robert finally let them make contact. He stood in a bar till they came. The man nodded at Robert and the girl laughed. He liked the girl; she looked tough with good hard features. Robert said, 'What do you want with me?'

'We're talent-spotters,' the man said.

'What line of business?' Robert said.

'You're speaking good Italian,' said the man, by which he meant that Robert was responding to the point.

In these days of their first acquaintance, the girl said very little. She was wonderfully lithe, wiry and coarse. Robert had never met anyone like her. She said her name was Anna and made the point that she never used a surname unless absolutely necessary, in which case she had a choice of surnames inscribed on a choice of documents and identification papers. Her uncle, who asked to be called Giorgio, was far more talkative. Giorgio was a butcher. Robert began to spend his afternoons and evenings with them, upstairs in their living-quarters above Giorgio's shop in a run-down alley, rowdy with barges. A sailors' bar, and a dingy barber's shop were the only commercial neighbours; it was impossible to tell if anyone lived behind the patched-up windows with an occasional box of geraniums in the upper storeys.

It was probably the first time in Robert's life that he had begun to understand himself, so warmly, and with what enthusiasm did he take to Giorgio and Anna. After his first meeting at the bar there followed a meal at their upstairs flat, cooked by Anna. Giorgio did nothing but talk at this time, and Robert listened, enthralled.

'I could write a novel about this,' Robert said.

'Go ahead,' said Giorgio.

Robert began to make himself at home in that little dingy room above the butcher's shop. Giorgio disappeared occasionally to see his customers when there were too many for his assistant to cope with, or when a barge arrived with a delivery of meat. Robert watched from the window while Giorgio and his man helped to carry a carcass of veal ashore on their shoulders.

He was delighted with the plan to extract big money from Curran, assuring his friends that Curran had millions and to spare.

Giorgio was less sure that the plan would work. 'People with millions don't always want to give it away.'

'Then you, yourself, were the actual Butcher who sliced up Pancev?' Robert said, smiling so openly and sunnily that his mother herself would have been amazed at the transformation.

'I was the apprentice. I was there in the garden to lend a hand. The master butcher's dead and I took over the business. Now, did you read in the papers about that butcher in Florence?'

'Tell me,' said Robert.

'Well, perhaps it was before you came to Italy. The butcher in Florence made a mess of it because he took a woman for a kidnap job, but they killed her before her husband could pay up. They dug her grave somewhere visible in the country, the fools, and killed her at the graveside. So they're in for life. But it struck me,' said Giorgio, 'that I've been too kind to those women at the Pensione Sofia all these years. And Curran, so rich, he must have known that sooner or later he'd have to pay. Times have changed. I've got my niece to provide for. She's a lovely girl. She's had a hard life and a bit of jail, but now we can possibly make things better for ourselves.'

Robert was equally forthcoming about the sad factors of his life. His bitterness in Paris with so many mean friends who wanted a pretty boy cheap and sometimes for nothing. Then Curran. 'And what have I got out of it?'

'You have your life in front of you,' said the Butcher.

All this time Anna would put cassettes into the player, so there was a constant background of music among the clatter of barges from outside in the canal and the loud voices of sailors from the bar. She weighed out a little cocaine mixed with something else on a piece of paper laid gently on a small letter-scale when someone she knew came to the door for it, but Robert approvingly noticed that they never touched the stuff themselves nor offered him any. They were serious people.

He told them anecdotes about his life with Curran, and before that, about Ambrose College and the snooping he had been able to do even after he had left school, by the simple means of having copies made of the house-master's keys.

'You know,' said Robert, 'I snooped. I got information. I never stole.'

'A real professional!' Giorgio said. 'Do you hear him, Anna? He's not a piddling pilferer. He's a born professional, this boy.'

They sat enjoying their conversations in the room above the butcher's shop so much that Robert, that week before he disappeared, was overwhelmed by gloom whenever he had to leave, to meet Lina, or to return to his room in the Pensione Sofia.

They decided he should disappear one afternoon. He had made the notes for his novel and it was Anna who suggested he should leave them on his table at the Pensione. 'An *avertimento*,' she said, showing her teeth as she spoke. She meant by this a warning of what was to come. Robert felt it only honourable to say, 'I can't guarantee that Curran will pay anything. He doesn't care a damn about me, at heart. He might just clear off.'

'He cares about his good name,' said Giorgio. 'People as wealthy as that can't easily hide.'

'How can I hide? They'll know where I am, for sure. Won't they come and find me here?' Robert said.

'We have a good hide-out. I rented it out two or three times to the kidnap business,' Giorgio said. 'What can Curran do, and *la* de Winter? They can't prove I was the apprentice who helped the old Butcher. I've got nothing to fear. I could make an anonymous call to the police. You see, *figlio mio*, they have the body in the garden, sliced in two. That's concrete. Everything else is anything you like.'

Robert and Anna laughed hilariously, and Anna changed the cassette. 'Let's say Curran killed Pancev,' said Robert.

Giorgio sat in the most comfortable chair in the room, a new Swedish-built leather chair with a foot-rest. He relaxed in the general ambience of friendliness; Robert felt he had known them all his life and told them so.

'It was a sight not to be missed,' said Giorgio, 'when we arrived at the garden that night. Here is the Countess de Winter waiting at the gate and Curran, very severe. As a young man Curran was very severe. He was a captain, lieutenant, something. So he stands there. Then the two girls, Katerina and Eufemia, are crying over the body. Katerina tries artificial respiration; she gets on top of him, working his arms. There is a towel on his wound, all bloody. Eufemia pulls her sister off him, turns him over, and gets astride him, pumping him like she was doing the week's washing. He is already much too dead. Then Katerina gets on top of him too . . .' Giorgio's words faded into a collapse of laughter with the younger people.

That Thursday afternoon when Robert was last seen talking to this middle-aged man and young woman outside the Santa Maria Formosa he had only a slight hesitation. He hadn't expected them to have arranged his disappearance so soon. He had planned to call in at the butcher's shop later in the day, to sit and laugh with them as usual. But they had followed him all morning. He had picked up an American girl student in the public water-bus to the other end of the island only to show his new friends that he was, after all, independent.

Then, when he could no longer avoid them, he went up to them and said, 'Well? See you later.'

'Better come now,' said Anna. She gave a vulgar snort which went to Robert's head, so enchanting he thought it.

On the way, as he accompanied them quite openly in the public water-bus to the other end of the island he thought: I could be walking into a trap.

He was still wary when he got to the butcher's shop and followed his friends upstairs to their sitting-room, thinking again: Am I walking into a trap? But he followed. And yet, when he finally reached the special room that was to be his hide-out, he immediately thought to himself: At last I'm home – I'm out of the trap.

But before he reached this room they had first entered into a high, floor-to-ceiling wall-safe opened by numerical code; it was a fairly large cupboard. They left Robert here for only a few minutes. He looked around and could see that the safe contained nothing of extreme value; for Robert, after spending two years with Curran's treasures, had a sense of these things. It looked very like the treasure-house of a hard-working trades-man. It contained some real silver trinkets set on velvet-lined shelves, some rustic old pieces of copper and bronze, pieces of furniture which might be original and only valuable if they were considered as good bargains picked up at some country dealer's, an old church tabernacle, probably of the sixteenth century. Curran-trained Robert took note of these things as he stood waiting, still a little uneasy. Anna had put on a cassette so he could not hear what she and Giorgio were saying to each other. He looked round the door. They waved him back, smiling so kindly at him that he felt foolish. Giorgio said, 'One moment, Roberto. You're not frightened, are you?'

Robert went back to his perusal of the spacious cupboard. A silver-plated kettle set on a little spirit-stove, about a hundred years old; an ivory inlaid desk; a Chinese lacquered screen. That these things were, in aggregate, a costly pile of junk still did not quite justify the intricate combination-code by which the deep high chamber was entered. Nothing really of interest to Christie's; and then it came to Robert that this was just such a plausible collection as the police might find, and count harmless, if they were looking for a hostage. When Giorgio and Anna joined him, beaming with delight, Robert put this theory to them.

'You're a marvel,' said Giorgio. 'You're born to the trade. I told you I was a talent-spotter.' He shifted aside a pianola from the far wall. 'That instrument functions, it plays,' said Anna. This was while Robert was still nagging himself: Am I walking into a trap? But Giorgio had moved a sliding door which led into the spacious room which was to be Robert's hide-out. It was the moment he walked into it that the thought came to him, with a rush of pleasure: At last I'm home – I'm out of the trap.

It was the beginning of Robert's happy days, the fine fruition of his youth. The windows of the room were boarded up and most of the time there was very little light as Giorgio did not want anything suspicious to show from the outside; he was careful to watch for creaks in the boards that shut up the windows. The room had been inhabited recently. It had a bed, a sofa, a wash-basin, a lavatory-bucket, an electric stove and a small table-lamp which they only lit late at night when they were drafting Robert's letters. 'Put in anything and everything,' Giorgio advised, 'and what you don't know, make up.' Another time, Giorgio said, 'What I'm telling you is true, or as near as. There are things those people won't even admit to themselves after thirty-five years of putting it behind them. They think they've become different persons.' To Robert, this activity was the most heavenly experience he had ever known. He and Anna made love whenever they wanted to. Giorgio seemed very pleased about this. 'It isn't everyone Anna falls in love with,' he told Robert, who was almost as delighted by this piece of information as he was by Giorgio's reports that by the look of things Robert's notes and letters had got 'them' all hopping.

Robert lost count of the days and nights. His friends came and had wonderful dinners with wine ... 'What time is it?' Robert said, once. 'Two in the morning,' said Giorgio.

Not that he cared. He could not have known, if they had not told him, that it was the sixth night when he went out with Anna to watch Lina dancing on her father's grave. They had planned it carefully, and the plan succeeded even better than Robert had expected. The sight of his father dancing there with Lina was a special joy to him. For Anna, the sight of Lina sufficed, for she had been suspicious of the Bulgarian girl, and was very relieved that Robert had shown such beautiful harshness towards her.

It was Thursday night, a week since Robert's disappearance. Curran had been to the Casino to try to take his mind off Robert. Earlier in the day he had followed Violet's instructions carefully. They were quite simple. He was to transfer from a bank in Switzerland half a million dollars to a numbered account in another bank in Switzerland. The transaction would be completed the next day.

'Are you sure that will be the end of it?' Curran asked her.

'Oh, yes.'

'How did they get hold of the bit about my being a German agent? Nobody knows the facts. It's not so easy as people might think. You and Riccardo . . .'

'We were different people then,' Violet said. 'Everything was different. Everyone else was different.'

'We're the same people,' Curran said. 'Any other point of view is foolish. We wouldn't be vulnerable if we were not the same people.'

He walked back through the cold night to the hotel from the Casino, convinced, as he always was when he had lost, that the tables had been rigged. It was after one o'clock. He looked forward to leaving Venice. He saw the smiling man as soon as he entered the hotel. The man turned, went into the lift and disappeared. Curran went to the reception desk and said to the clerk, 'What is that gentleman's name?'

'A Signor Bee,' said the clerk.

'How do you spell it?'

The clerk looked up the register, and spelt it for Curran.

'Where does he come from?'

'An address in Lisbon, from the passport.'

When Curran came down in the morning he saw the smiler once more. It was only a glimpse. The man was sitting in the bay window of the lobby which looked out over the great lagoon. It was a day of wind and sunshine and a number of sailing boats were taking advantage of the favourable weather; there was probably a race in progress. On the table where the smiler sat, a few little white cards were assembled. Curran felt suddenly terrified and left the hotel right away.

When he got to Violet's house he said, 'That B. of yours is staying at my hotel. He's playing with paper boats, sitting there, taunting me, with half a million of my money already in his bank.'

Violet said, 'Oh, has it gone through? Have you heard from Switzerland this morning?'

'Yes,' he said.

'Well, thank God for that. I haven't slept. There's only one little thing, Mr B. told me you have to do some little thing for the Butcher, who's very disappointed. But something quite negligible like a hundred thousand—'

'Negligible!' said Curran. 'Do you think it grows on trees? This will go on and on. There's no end to it.'

'No,' said Violet. 'Pay the Butcher. I swear it is the end. I'll tell you precisely what you must do . . .'

It was before dawn that Giorgio had woken up his niece and Robert from their deep and interlocked sleep in the hide-out, but to Robert it might have been any time of the day. Giorgio was frantic.

'Get up and get out, both of you,' Giorgio had said. 'Out of Venice and away. I'll give you money and any identification documents you like but you've got to go. The Big Five are on to us; they've sent one of their men to Venice and he's taken over. Get yourselves dressed and out. If you're still in

Venice by daylight we'll be all three of us at the bottom of the lagoon at nightfall.'

Before they left, Anna turned on Giorgio. 'Bourgeois capitalist cringer,' she said. 'You'll get a big cut out of this, won't you?'

They were out of Venice, Anna and Robert, far inland on what the Venetians call *terra ferma*, by the first train. By eight o'clock that morning they sat having their coffee and rolls in a bar in Verona.

Arnold was having a late breakfast in the dining-room of the Hotel Lord Byron. He had finished his half-grapefruit and his cornflakes and was now eating his English bacon and eggs which the hotel made a point of offering its Anglo-Saxon guests. He was trying to decipher an Italian newspaper; he had said 'Buon giorno' to all and sundry, and was generally minding his own business when he was approached by a tall, lean, dark young man who looked at him in a fierce way.

'Buon giorno,' said Arnold, taking off his reading spectacles and putting on his looking ones.

'You want to know what's good for you?' said the young man.

'What?' said Arnold.

'You leave my girl alone, you dirty old man.'

'With whom,' said Arnold, 'am I talking and to whom do you refer?'

'I'm Serge Pancev, second cousin and fiancé of Lina Pancev. You come from London? I've been in London. I know the quality of person that you are.'

'My dear young man, I've only taken an interest in the

poor girl, a refugee from the Iron Curtain and the oppression of her co-nationals. I am a former headmaster and I do think it behoves us to show some charity to these strangers in our midst.'

'I like to know what you mean by the oppression of her co-nationals,' Serge said. 'I like an explanation. As a co-national and a cousin.'

'I understand,' Arnold said. 'I think in cases like this we must call for a compromise. What are you doing out here, by the way?'

'I've come for Lina and I'm going to take her back.'

'I'm a married man, myself,' Arnold said, 'so you see, I understand your point of view.'

'You don't ask her to any more fancy dinners and fancy lunches,' stated Serge.

'I hope she won't get into trouble in her country,' said Arnold.

Serge banged his fist on the table to the effect that the lid of the metal coffee-pot sprung open as if its hair was standing on end, and a spurt of coffee splashed from its spout on to the white tablecloth.

'I hope,' said Serge, 'that you won't get into trouble, yourself, when you return to your own territory.'

' . . . a spirit of compromise,' Arnold was saying. 'I haven't been a headmaster of a boys' school all these years without knowing something . . . '

Serge was already leaving the dining-room, and the waiter stepped forward to place a clean napkin over the coffee-stains on the tablecloth.

Arnold went to the desk clerk and sent off a wire to Anthea: 'Beautiful weather here home next week Arnold.'

16

It was the next day, Saturday, before Curran could get together enough dollar currency to satisfy the Butcher's precise demands as they were relayed to him by Violet. All of Friday afternoon he had been ringing up his lawyers and banks. Violet had told him that Italian lire were out of the question, too traceable and too likely to be false; and still, in the early evening of Friday when the arrangements were complete, there was another crisis, a hitch. Violet had received a phone call to say that the Butcher wanted deutschmarks after all. But it all blew over, and after some more cautiously worded phone calls it was agreed that Curran would take his pay-off dollars to the altar of Santa Barbara at the Church of Santa Maria Formosa at five o'clock precisely the next day.

Punctually then, on Saturday, Curran was in the church with a briefcase in his hand, and an angry throbbing in his ears and in the region of what he felt to be his thyroid gland. The church was dark and still. An old woman prayed at the altar of the large and predominantly red Sànta Barbara.

Curran knelt before Santa Barbara. The old woman moved away and dragged slowly round the church, muttering her own secrets to herself or to God or whatever. Curran then caught sight of the Butcher, and although he had seen him frequently with the young blonde woman since he had come to Venice, this was the first time that Curran felt he recognized in the puffy face and thickened shoulders the features of that young apprentice of the summer night of 1945, there in the garden of the Pensione Sofia, getting down to business with the older butcher.

Curran put his briefcase on the floor in front of Santa Barbara, and started to leave the church casually, looking here and there, as a sightseer. He noticed that the Butcher was loitering at an altar at the back of the church beside the small dark stylized painting of the Madonna. Curran hurried to the entrance of the church quite sure that his business was settled. The old woman was still roaming around and the Butcher had not moved. Curran then noticed another woman, in a shawl, standing in the shadows of the first alcove near the door: Lina Pancev, the last person Curran wanted to be bothered with.

Lina skipped forward to confront him. 'I looked for you this morning at your hotel,' she said. 'I have to tell you that your friend Violet is so mean to me, it—'

'Look, I'm in a hurry,' Curran said. 'You have to excuse me.'

'You hear from Robert?'

'No, nothing at all.'

'I come here to this church every evening to look for Robert. He—'

But Curran was gone.

Outside a number of people were running. These were the family and friends of someone who had been taken ill and who was being carried by two hospital men, Venetian style, in a chair to the hospital-boat which awaited them at the canal. Curran dodged the puffing group, so old, some of these people, that they themselves seemed to be risking a heart attack. Eventually Curran got ahead of the procession, so that he did not notice that Lina was pursuing him, as best she could, among the anxious relatives of the sick person. Lina was indeed trying to catch up with Curran; she had his briefcase in her hand, under the impression he had forgotten it.

By the time the invalid and some of the crowd of friends had packed themselves into the ambulance-boat, Curran had disappeared. There were several alleys and waterways leading from this point, but Lina couldn't see him anywhere. The remaining relatives of the sick person were excitedly arranging for another boat to take them after their stricken one. Lina stood among them, still looking around her. Her arm was then wrenched by a middle-aged man with a puffy face whom she seemed to recognize, but as he was without his usual companion, the blonde girl, she failed exactly to place him as the man who had been cropping up so frequently in her path and Robert's. She said, 'What are you doing?'

'Give me that bag.'

'I will not. Don't touch me. I'll call the police. This bag belongs to a friend of mine. I saw him leave it behind in the church.'

The man tugged at the briefcase. Lina shouted 'No!' and started an eloquent appeal to the people around her, to the boatmen who had just arrived with their water-taxis and to the skies. She peppered her protest with plenty of demands for the police, then she got into a boat with some of the people, leaving the man still protesting on the landing-stage.

'Well, Arnold,' said Grace, 'I just popped round to see how you are. You must be lonely without Mary. But can you blame her?' Leo was smiling by her side.

'Mary is entitled to lead her own life, whatever she's up to. I'm on my holidays, Grace, *if* you please.'

'Such things are going on in Italy,' Grace said, sitting down beside him in the hall of the Hotel Lord Byron. She pointed to another vacant chair. 'Sit down, Leo,' she said. 'Leo,' she said, 'has been translating the news for me. It's worse than London. Look at this.' She put a newspaper down on the table open on the second page, and pointed to a headline with underneath it the police identikit of a young man and a young woman. They looked stylized, almost Byzantine in the photokit drawing.

'I've seen the paper this morning,' said Arnold. 'There's always crime. I like the real news.'

'Young boy and girl rob jeweller in Verona,' Grace said. 'Jeweller seriously wounded. And that's the identikit that the witnesses put together. Both got away. Stolen car.'

Arnold gave only a passing glance at the pictures lying before him on the page.

'Must have been a fast car,' said Leo.

'I'll be going home next week,' said Arnold.

'Well, that's nice. I'll tell Anthea when I ring tomorrow.'

'Naturally I've already sent her a telegram,' said Arnold.

'Well,' said Grace, 'we'd better be trotting along. Just a bit like Robert, that photo, isn't it?'

'Robert? Nothing like Robert. All these students look alike.'

Grace and Leo left, and Arnold took off his looking spectacles and put on his reading ones.

Robert and Anna stood at a bar in Padova. A dark, small young man came up to Robert. 'Hallo,' he said.

'What do you want?' said Robert.

'Your documents, please.'

'Who are you? Carabinieri?'

'That's right.'

'*Your* documents, please,' Robert said.

The man showed his police identification. Robert and Anna then showed their papers: Robert without his moustache and Anna with her hair cut short and dyed brown, just as they looked at that moment. They were James Rooke of Taunton, Devon, and Maria Graziella Lotti of Milan.

The policeman let well alone. The bar was crowded.

Shortly afterwards they were approached by an older man.

'Who are you?' said Robert.

'A talent spotter,' said the man. 'You can depend on us.

We can give you guarantees. Let me congratulate you both. Precise, quick-limbed, beautiful style. We can offer you a future.'

Lina took Curran's briefcase back to the Ca' Winter, for she had an appointment there with Serge. She intended to take him with her to Curran's hotel and to make this thoughtful restitution of his briefcase the occasion for a long complaint against Violet, who was expecting her to do work which was less than *au pair*. When she got to her studio Lina thought she had better look inside, just to see what was there: dollars, one-hundred-dollar bills, fifty-dollar bills, in all one hundred and fifty thousand dollars. She stacked them neatly back into the briefcase, put it on her bed and sat down beside it, very still, waiting for Serge.

She immediately told him how she had found the briefcase left behind in the church by Curran.

'What were you doing in the church?'

'Looking round for my boy-friend Robert, to give him a big goodbye. It is a nice church, besides. I think perhaps my father went there to pray. Look what is in the briefcase.'

'American money,' he said.

'To think that he carried it round with him,' she said. 'It makes me sick.'

'Bourgeois capitalist pig,' said Serge.

'He buys the boys and the girls with it. Then I can't tell you how I had to struggle with a man who wanted to steal it. The man must have known it was full of money.'

'What you going to do with it?' Serge said.

'Take it to Curran at his hotel and hand it over and spit on him.'

Serge seemed to think that she might be entitled to keep the money since this would really only be an act of proletarian re-appropriation, but Lina said, 'Maybe it's a trap.'

They did take the briefcase full of bank-notes to Curran at his hotel. Lina told him how she had nearly been killed trying to protect it.

All Curran said was, 'You should have let the man take it. There's nothing much inside.' And he went off, wearily, to make a telephone call, with the briefcase in his hand, and not so much as a good-evening to Serge or a thank-you to her.

Arnold, on Sunday morning, sat at his breakfast. On the front page of his newspaper was an article about a bank robbery at Bologna. Again, the photokits of the two suspects, described as '*I Bonnie e Clyde d'Italia*'. Apparently they had robbed a bank, killing a customer and a policeman before getting away with a gigantic haul. Arnold turned to the next page.

Anthea was reading her novel, on Sunday evening, but impatiently, for she was hoping that Grace would ring her from Venice. For once, she had information for Grace rather than the other way round.

Matt pushed the second beer-can over to Colin. As he took a draught from his own can, he mumbled, 'I guess this had to happen.'

The stained check tablecloth lay between them like an accusation.

Colin looked at Matt for a long moment. 'Did you know that Beryl's taken a job in a sort of beauty-parlour?'

'Christ! What does that mean?'

'It's a way out.'

'Beauty-parlour? What's beautiful about it?'

Matt took a long draught of beer. 'That's the way it is,' he said after a long silence.

The telephone rang. 'Oh, Grace, it's you. I can hear you just as if you were in the next room. I've got news, Grace.'

'Arnold's going home Monday or Tuesday,' Grace said. 'And he sent you a telegram.'

'Oh, yes, Arnold. Well, I've got more news than that. This morning there was a ring at the bell. I looked at the clock. Only five past nine. I thought to myself: Who can that be at this hour on a Sunday morning? Well I went to the door and there was a man with a small package for me. He said he was an airline steward, friend of Robert. I asked him to come in but he wouldn't, he had to be on his way. I could see his car at the door, very smart and sporty. Anyway he left me this package, he said from Robert. Well, Grace, I opened the packet and what do you think? You'll never believe, it was a diamond and sapphire bracelet, a present for me, with a lovely, very lovely note from Robert. He's got a fine job as a travel executive and he says he's going to stick to it. You never saw such a lovely bracelet in your life. I'm so thrilled and, Grace, the relief of it all. I never said so, but I was always afraid he was unhappy and involved in some wrong-doing.'

'You're mistaken if you think wrong-doers are always unhappy,' Grace said. 'The really professional evil-doers love it. They're as happy as larks in the sky. I wasn't a Matron all those years without finding out a thing or two about human nature.'

'Oh, Grace, all I want to say is I'm thankful Robert's not in bad company and unhappy. It's the most lovely present I ever had. I don't know how much—'

'The unhappy ones are only the guilty amateurs and the neurotics,' said Grace. 'The pros are in their element.' The telephone buzzed and crackled.

'I don't hear what you're saying, Grace. It's difficult on the phone. I hope to see Robert again soon. He doesn't say, but—'

'You'll be seeing Arnold soon,' Grace said.

'What's happened to the student girl? I've been thinking it over. Was she the same foreign girl that Robert took up with?'

'That's right. You're a good guesser, Anthea. It was a very paternal relationship, Anthea. The girl – well, I say "girl" but she's no spring chicken – is going back to her own country. It's behind the Iron Curtain but her boy-friend's a party boss so he can make it all right for her. In fact she told me they'll welcome her with open arms.'

Anthea seemed to gather that a party boss meant a master of ceremonies at a dance, but she was not much interested in this foreign girl, and the line continued to crackle. She started to give Grace a better description of the diamond and sapphire bracelet until Grace interrupted, saying she was going to an evening mass, for the experience and the atmosphere, with Leo, who always translated the sermons for her.

'But Grace, don't tell Arnold about the bracelet. I want it to be a surprise,' Anthea shouted.

'That's right. And the last time I went to a service here in Venice there was a sermon about birth control that Leo translated for me under his breath. I don't know why the RC Church doesn't stick to politics and keep its nose out of morals.'

'I'll let you see it when you come home, Grace. It's the most lovely bracelet.'

'Yes, a lovely holiday. Venice is fantastic, lovely.'

In bed, in her dreams, came Anthea's Ayrshire grandmother with her song:

> There's a youth in this city, it were a great pity,
> > That he from our lasses should wander awa;
> For he's bonie and braw ...
>
> > Weel-featur'd, weel-tocher'd, weel-mounted and
> > > braw;
> But chiefly the siller, that gars him gang till her,
> > The pennie's the jewel that beautifies a'.
> > > ... the pennie's the jewel ...
> > > ... the jewel ...

17

Robert and Anna were having a drink in a bar in Trieste, smiling at each other. A middle-aged man in a business suit approached them.

'What do you want?' Robert said.

'I'm a talent-spotter. You two have got everything. You've got style. You can make the top.'

As a result of this meeting Robert and Anna were sent to the Middle East to train in a terrorist camp.

Lina returned to Bulgaria with Serge where she was put to happy use as a first-rate example of a repentant dissident, the moment, besides, being right. News of her re-defection was loudly proclaimed in the western papers and she was encouraged to give interviews to the journalists of all nations on the theme of western decadence and all the vicissitudes of her life in Paris and Venice. She described her tumble-down flat. She described the slave-driving Countess who forbade her to eat meat and gave her no time to do her paintings. She bewailed her father's grave, which she had never found. She told of the elderly American millionaire who went about with a brief-case full of dollars seducing young people of both sexes.

Curran saw that his briefcase got into the hands it was destined for; then he went to India to see his guru.

Violet persuaded Leo to take over the fine studio at the top of her house and to join her in launching a tourist project called 'Venice by Night'. Leo became an excellent travel executive and did well for himself and Violet.

Arnold, on his return to Birmingham, was greatly relieved to find Anthea in a good humour, indeed in a state of excitement. She showed him Robert's diamond and sapphire bracelet.

'You always thought he had no heart,' she said.

'Oh, I wouldn't say that. He was always kind to animals, don't forget.'

Grace Gregory and Mary Tiller went on a round-the-world tour together in search of adventures which made Mary feel agreeably guilty and Grace happily conscious of the comparative innocence of her own past life.

Katerina and Eufemia were always busy in the Pensione Sofia, whether attending to their guests at all seasons of the year or cultivating their roses in the garden, beyond which the canals lapped on the sides of the banks, the palaces of Venice rode in great state and the mosaics stood with the same patience that had gone into their formation, piece by small piece.